Lung cancer
33996002142669

Laguna Vista Public Library
1300 Palm Blvd.
Laguna Vista, TX 78578

DISEASES & DISORDERS

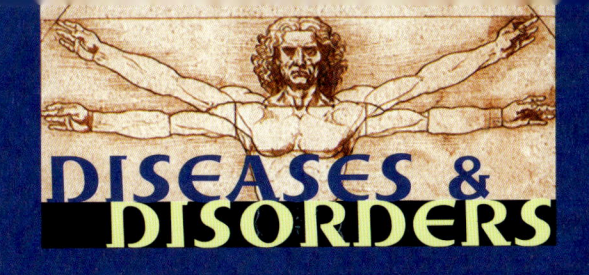

Lung Cancer

Barbara Sheen

LUCENT BOOKS
An imprint of Thomson Gale, a part of The Thomson Corporation

THOMSON
GALE

Detroit • New York • San Francisco • New Haven, Conn. • Waterville, Maine • London

THOMSON
━━━━★━━━━ ™
GALE

© 2008 Thomson Gale, a part of The Thomson Corporation.

Thomson and Star Logo are trademarks and Gale and Lucent Books are registered trademarks used herein under license.

For more information, contact
Lucent Books
27500 Drake Rd.
Farmington Hills, MI 48331-3535
Or you can visit our Internet site at http://www.gale.com

ALL RIGHTS RESERVED.
No part of this work covered by the copyright hereon may be reproduced or used in any form or by any means—graphic, electronic, or mechanical, including photocopying, recording, taping, Web distribution or information storage retrieval systems—without the written permission of the publisher.

Every effort has been made to trace the owners of copyrighted material.

Library of Congress Cataloging-in-Publication Data

Sheen, Barbara.
  Lung cancer / by Barbara Sheen.
    p. cm. -- (Diseases and disorders)
  Includes bibliographical references and index.
  ISBN 978-1-4205-0043-1 (hardcover)
  1. Lungs--Cancer--Juvenile literature. I. Title.
  RC280.L8S523 2008
  616.99'424--dc22
                                                    2007040392

ISBN-10: 1-4205-0043-0
Printed in the United States of America

Table of Contents

Foreword   4

Introduction:
   The Forgotten Cancer   6

Chapter One:
   What is Lung Cancer?   11

Chapter Two:
   Symptoms and Diagnosis   27

Chapter Three:
   Treatment   41

Chapter Four:
   Living with Lung Cancer   55

Chapter Five:
   What the Future Holds   70

Notes   86

Glossary   92

Organizations to Contact   95

For Further Reading   97

Index   99

Picture Credits   104

About the Author   104

FOREWORD

"The Most Difficult Puzzles Ever Devised"

Charles Best, one of the pioneers in the search for a cure for diabetes, once explained what it is about medical research that intrigued him so. "It's not just the gratification of knowing one is helping people," he confided, "although that probably is a more heroic and selfless motivation. Those feelings may enter in, but truly, what I find best is the feeling of going toe to toe with nature, of trying to solve the most difficult puzzles ever devised. The answers are there somewhere, those keys that will solve the puzzle and make the patient well. But how will those keys be found?"

Since the dawn of civilization, nothing has so puzzled people—and often frightened them, as well—as the onset of illness in a body or mind that had seemed healthy before. A seizure, the inability of a heart to pump, the sudden deterioration of muscle tone in a small child—being unable to reverse such conditions or even to understand why they occur was unspeakably frustrating to healers. Even before there were names for such conditions, even before they were understood at all, each was a reminder of how complex the human body was, and how vulnerable.

Foreword

While our grappling with understanding diseases has been frustrating at times, it has also provided some of humankind's most heroic accomplishments. Alexander Fleming's accidental discovery in 1928 of a mold that could be turned into penicillin has resulted in the saving of untold millions of lives. The isolation of the enzyme insulin has reversed what was once a death sentence for anyone with diabetes. There have been great strides in combating conditions for which there is not yet a cure, too. Medicines can help AIDS patients live longer, diagnostic tools such as mammography and ultrasound can help doctors find tumors while they are treatable, and laser surgery techniques have made the most intricate and minute operations routine.

This "toe-to-toe" competition with diseases and disorders is even more remarkable when seen in a historical continuum. An astonishing amount of progress has been made in a very short time. Just two hundred years ago, the existence of germs as a cause of some diseases was unknown. In fact, it was less than 150 years ago that a British surgeon named Joseph Lister had difficulty persuading his fellow doctors that washing their hands before delivering a baby might increase the chances of a healthy delivery (especially if they had just attended to a diseased patient)!

Each book in Lucent's Diseases and Disorders series explores a disease or disorder and the knowledge that has been accumulated (or discarded) by doctors through the years. Each book also examines the tools used for pinpointing a diagnosis, as well as the various means that are used to treat or cure a disease. Finally, new ideas are presented—techniques or medicines that may be on the horizon.

Frustration and disappointment are still part of medicine, for not every disease or condition can be cured or prevented. But the limitations of knowledge are being pushed outward constantly; the "most difficult puzzles ever devised" are finding challengers every day.

INTRODUCTION

The Forgotten Cancer

Lung cancer is the deadliest form of cancer known to man. It kills more Americans each year than colon, prostate, breast, liver, and kidney cancers combined. Yet the disease gets little coverage in the media and less research funding than many less lethal illnesses. Because lung cancer is associated with smoking, there is a stigma attached to the disease. This influences the way the public looks at it, as well as the way people with the disease are treated by others. Many lung cancer patients say that they are made to feel like they are to blame for their illness

Although smoking is the main cause of lung cancer, it is not the only cause of the disease.

and are, therefore, less deserving of support and sympathy than individuals with other conditions. "Lung cancer is thought of as something you bring on yourself," says Glen, a lung cancer survivor. "I could see that in the faces of some of the people when I told them. One person said to me, 'You smoked like a chimney—what did you expect?' I thought that was cruel, but I let it go. I'm more interested in living than in the small stuff."[1]

While it is true that smoking is the predominant cause of lung cancer, it is not the only cause. Moreover, many other diseases are linked to unhealthy lifestyle choices but there is no stigma attached to them. For instance, alcohol consumption causes liver disease. And, smoking, poor diet, and inactivity contributes to heart disease as well as many types of cancer. People who contract these conditions are less often made to feel that their illness is self-inflicted. Karen Parles, a lung cancer survivor, author, and creator of Lung Cancer Online Foundation, a lung cancer advocacy organization, has this to say:

> A constant reminder of the smoking stigma associated with this disease is the inevitable question I hear when someone learns I have lung cancer, "Did you smoke…?" Despite having never smoked, I still resent what is implied by the question, and wonder why people with coronary artery [heart] disease aren't confronted in the same way.[2]

Lack of Attention

Unlike other forms of cancer, lung cancer garners little media attention. This is unfortunate because print, broadcast, and online coverage are among the best ways to garner public support for an issue and to disseminate information to the public. "There is a tremendous ignorance about the facts of lung cancer," says Deborah Morosini, MD, the sister of actress Dana Reeves, a non-smoker, who died of lung cancer in 2006. "Even I, as a physician who works in research every day was unaware of the facts until I had to face Dana's tragedy."[3]

Most Americans do not know that lung cancer is the most common form of cancer in men, worldwide, and the second most common in women. Or that in the United States alone, 13 percent of all new cancer cases are caused by lung cancer, as are 28 percent of all cancer deaths. That translates to 170,000 new lung cancer cases annually and 160,000 deaths. What is even more troubling is that, although overall cancer rates are declining, the incidence of lung cancer in American women is on the rise, particularly among non-smokers. Indeed, lung cancer is now the leading cause of cancer deaths in American women.

The stigma attached to the disease also contributes to the lack of public support for lung cancer patients. Parles observes:

> Seasoned lung cancer advocates tell countless stories of approaching celebrities to speak out against lung cancer. Time after time, celebrities refuse to participate in lung cancer events because they don't want to be associated with a "smoker's disease." The most striking evidence of the apathy towards those afflicted with lung cancer is the virtual nonexistence of awareness and fundraising events... There are no walk-a-thons, no golf outings, no wine tastings, no hospital gala events benefiting lung cancer research, or funding support services for people with lung cancer. Television, radio, and newspaper outlets offer special features on breast, ovarian, prostate, colon, and children's cancers, but virtually nothing on the number one cancer killer. This lack of public empathy and support is demoralizing—our personal battles against lung cancer are compounded by the added stigma of having a "smoker's disease."[4]

Limited Research Funds

Similarly, funding for lung cancer research is less than that for other cancers. In 2005, for example, funding for breast cancer research totaled 150 million dollars. Funds for prostate cancer topped 85 million dollars. In comparison, lung cancer

The Forgotten Cancer

Women participating in the Avon Breast Cancer 3-Day event. Unlike the public awareness campaigns that other cancers receive, lung cancer is often given little public attention or fundraising efforts.

received 2.1 million dollars. Lung cancer advocates say that this disparity is one reason that five-year survival rate of breast and prostate cancers have increased dramatically, while that of lung cancer has not changed significantly in decades. Looking at statistics, in 1976 the five-year survival rate for breast cancer was 75 percent. By 2000, it jumped to 88 percent. For prostate cancer those rates climbed from 67 to 96 percent. Lung cancer survival rates, on the other hand went from 13 to 15 percent. Sportscaster Joe Buck, whose father died of lung cancer, has this to say: "It [lung cancer] kills more people than all the major cancers, but remains the least funded. It's an unbelievable contradiction and one that needs to end now."[5]

Becoming Aware

Raising awareness of lung cancer is the best way to remove the stigma attached to the disease. That, in turn, should increase media coverage, public support, and research funding. Such actions have the potential to both reduce the incidence of new lung cancer cases and increase survival rates. Clearly, no one deserves a deadly disease. Becoming educated about lung cancer is one of the best ways to support lung cancer patients and their families. It can also help healthy individuals to take steps to lessen their risk of developing lung cancer.

Sandy Phillips Britt, a lung cancer patient, put it this way:

> At this point, no one survives Stage IV [the most advanced stage] lung cancer indefinitely. Until lung cancer starts being treated as a disease worthy of sympathy and support, instead of as a punishment, this will remain true. As those of us active in Lung Cancer Alliance, the nation's only nonprofit group dedicated solely to support and advocacy for people living with and at risk for the disease, say, "No more excuses. No more lung cancer." [It is] Too late for me, but maybe not for you or someone you love.[6]

Britt died of lung cancer in 2007.

CHAPTER ONE

What is Lung Cancer?

Lung cancer is a form of cancer that develops in a person's lungs, the organ necessary for breathing. In most cases exposure to carcinogens, chemicals with cancer causing properties, causes lung cancer—but not always. Lung cancer occurs when mutated cells on the surface of a lung, or in an airway leading to a lung, grow uncontrollably and without purpose. Besides compromising the lung's ability to function, these cells can break away from the lungs and spread throughout the body, which can be fatal. These two characteristics, the uncontrollable growth of cells and the ability of the cells to spread throughout the body, define cancer. When lung cells are involved, the result is lung cancer.

Uncontrollable Dividing Cells

The human body is made up of trillions of cells, each with a particular job to do. In a well-regulated process, cells grow, divide, and create more cells whenever the body needs them. For instance, when cells get old, they die and are replaced by new cells. Genes within each cell regulate this process by signaling the cells when it is time to divide and when it is time to stop. But sometimes, due to cell mutation, the process breaks and the signaling genes fail to function properly. When this happens, the mutated cells continuously divide even though new cells are not needed. Indeed, the sole function of the mutated cells is to divide. And, since they do not die like normal cells, they can, potentially, go on dividing forever. According to

The Lungs

Each day an individual breathes approximately 25,000 times. The lungs, two spongy organs located in the chest, make breathing possible.

When a person breathes, oxygen is inhaled through the nose or mouth and passes through a long hollow tube called the trachea or windpipe. The windpipe branches off into the airways or bronchi. These are two tubes that connect to each lung. Inside the lungs, the bronchi split into bronchiole, tiny tubes no larger than a strand of hair. At the end of the bronchioles are millions of small air sacs called alveoli that are surrounded by blood vessels. Oxygen crosses from the alveoli into the bloodstream via these blood vessels. At the same time, carbon dioxide passes out of the bloodstream to the alveoli. The process is reversed and the carbon dioxide is exhaled from the body.

A thin membrane called the pleura covers the surface of the lungs. It contains elastic tissue, which allows the organ to inflate and deflate as people breathe in and out.

Robert A. Weinberg, world-renowned cancer expert and the discoverer of the signaling genes involved in cell formation, "Normal cells are civic-minded, lining up together in a precise architecture that gives structure to body tissue. When the cell's genes are damaged, they send out faulty instructions, turning orderly structure into a chaotic mess."[7]

Malignant Tumors

As the mutated cells divide, they cram against each other and bump together forming an abnormal mass known as a malignant or cancerous tumor. Sometimes normal cells, too, bump together and form a mass. Such a mass is called a benign tumor. Benign tumors do not grow uncontrollably and are, therefore,

What is Lung Cancer?

not cancerous. A malignant tumor, on the other hand, grows unchecked. As it does, it crowds out normal cells, taking blood, nutrients, and oxygen away from them. This weakens the cells, compromising their ability to do their job, and eventually destroys them. At the same time, the tumor may block the airways, which makes breathing difficult. Malignant tumors, according to Weinberg, "have no interest in the well-being of the tissue and organism around them …. They have only one program in mind, more growth, more replicas of themselves, unlimited expansion."[8]

Making matters worse, despite the danger cancer cells pose, since cancer cells are mutated body cells, the immune system does not recognize them as harmful. Normally, when a foreign substance threatens the body, the immune system

An illustration showing how the human respiratory system works.

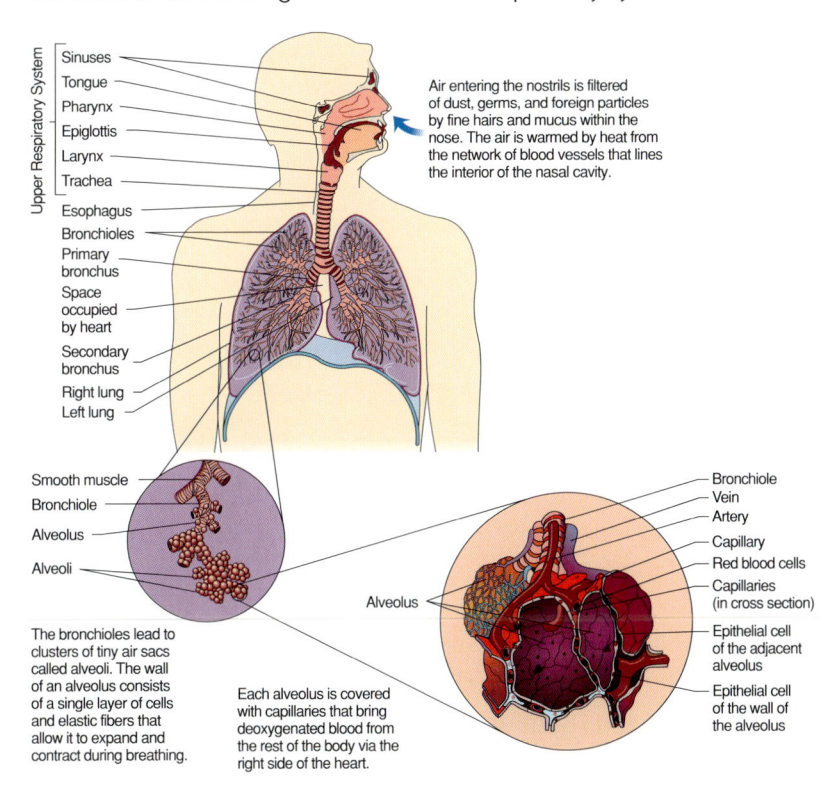

Upper Respiratory System
- Sinuses
- Tongue
- Pharynx
- Epiglottis
- Larynx
- Trachea
- Esophagus
- Bronchioles
- Primary bronchus
- Space occupied by heart
- Secondary bronchus
- Right lung
- Left lung

Air entering the nostrils is filtered of dust, germs, and foreign particles by fine hairs and mucus within the nose. The air is warmed by heat from the network of blood vessels that lines the interior of the nasal cavity.

- Smooth muscle
- Bronchiole
- Alveolus
- Alveoli

The bronchioles lead to clusters of tiny air sacs called alveoli. The wall of an alveolus consists of a single layer of cells and elastic fibers that allow it to expand and contract during breathing.

Alveolus

Each alveolus is covered with capillaries that bring deoxygenated blood from the rest of the body via the right side of the heart.

- Bronchiole
- Vein
- Artery
- Capillary
- Red blood cells
- Capillaries (in cross section)
- Epithelial cell of the adjacent alveolus
- Epithelial cell of the wall of the alveolus

sends out white blood cells and powerful chemicals to attack and destroy the threat. Cancer cells, however, are not a foreign substance. So the immune system treats cancer cells as if they were healthy body cells, leaving them free to grow unchecked and damage the body. Weinberg explains:

> Tumors are not foreign invaders. They arise from the same material the body uses to construct its own tissues. Tumors use the same components—human cells—to form the jumbled masses that disrupt biological order and function and, if left unchecked, to bring the whole complex life-sustaining edifice that is the human body crashing down.[9]

The Cancer Spreads

Without anything to check its growth, the tumor continues to enlarge. As it does, it moves into surrounding tissue, spreading throughout the lungs to the membrane that surrounds the organ and to the lining of the chest. "One of my most essential organs, my only access to life-sustaining oxygen had been invaded," explains Aaron, a man with lung cancer. "Something was in there—a big ominous round mass stationed in the middle of my otherwise healthy lung. To add to its insidiousness, it appears that it had replicated itself, sending off baby drones to the surrounding tissue and even sending one across the divide into my other lung"[10]

Worse yet, in a process called shedding, cancer cells break free from the tumor. Once this happens the cells are transported to other organs through the bloodstream and/or the lymphatic system, a network of thin tubes that carries white blood cells throughout the body. The cells then lodge themselves in distant organs where they grow, divide, and form new tumors. This process is known as metastasis. Lung cancer cells can spread to any part of the body, but they are most likely to lodge themselves in the brain, bones, liver, lymph nodes, and adrenal glands. Ed, a lung cancer survivor, says when his cancer was

What is Lung Cancer?

discovered he had: "tumors on my spine, ribs, neck, and collar bone… and large tumors on both adrenal glands."[11]

What makes lung cancer especially dangerous is its doubling time—that is, the time it takes for the cells to divide and double. Depending on the type of cancer, doubling time can be anywhere from 30 days to several years. Lung cancer cells are aggressive. Their doubling time is between 30 and 180 days. That means the disease has the potential to metastasize in a matter of months.

Carcinogens and Lung Cancer

Although lung cancer can develop spontaneously, most cases are caused by exposure to carcinogenic substances that damage lung tissue and lead to cell mutation. These include various inhaled toxins like tobacco smoke, radon, asbestos, and radiation, with exposure to cigarette smoke ranking number

In a process called shedding, cancer cells, like the one pictured here, break free from the tumor and are transported throughout the body in the bloodstream.

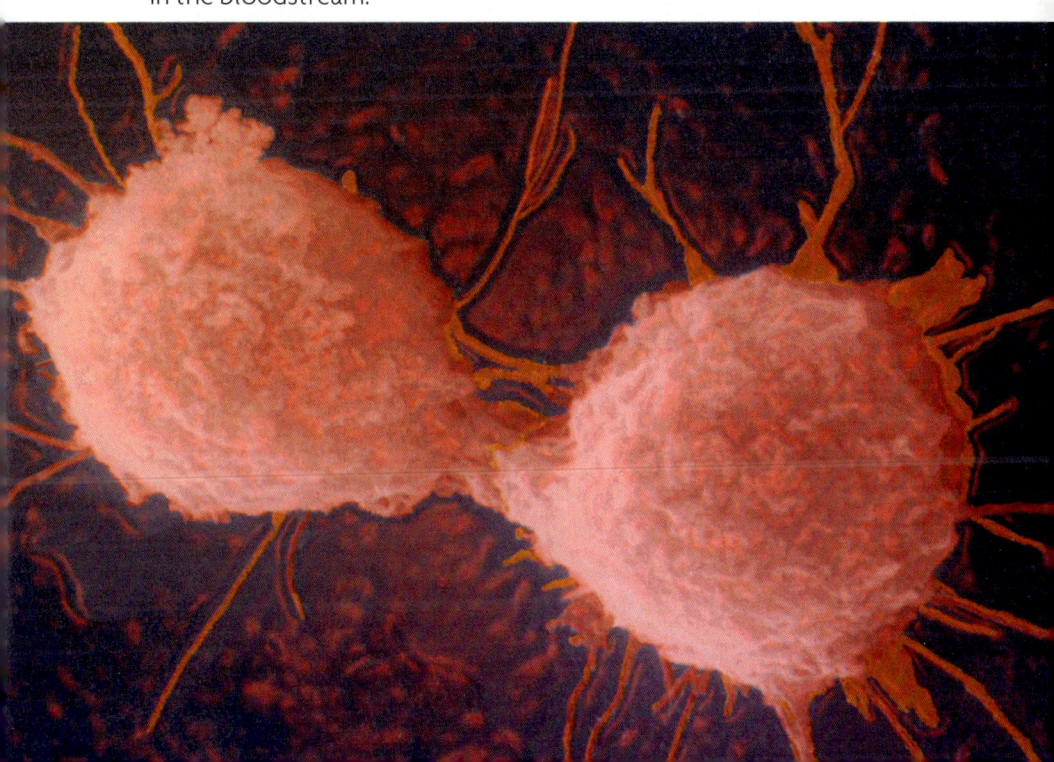

one. "Statistically," explains Ronald Natale, MD, of Cedar Sinai Cancer Institute, Los Angeles, "about one in eight smokers develop cancer—most of them lung cancer. So this is a dangerous habit."[12]

Tobacco smoke contains more than four thousand dangerous chemicals, fifty of which are known carcinogens. When people smoke these chemicals are transferred into the lungs. This transfer occurs because smoking harms the lungs' natural cleaning system. Normally, when chemicals, dirt, and other harmful substances get into a person's airways, mucus inside the airways traps the harmful substance. Then tiny hairs called cilia push it out. Smoking, however, damages and destroys cilia. As a result, dirt, dust, and chemicals from smoking lodge in the lungs, which makes lung cells more likely to mutate. As a matter of fact, the greater the build-up of these substances, the greater an individual's chances of developing lung cancer. Once cancer develops, nicotine in cigarette smoke appears to make matters worse, attaching to cancer cells and stimulating their growth.

With this in mind, it is not surprising that an estimated 90 percent of all lung cancer cases are smoking related. In fact, between 1964 and 2004, more than two million Americans died from smoking-related-lung cancer. According to the National Cancer Institute, the risk of developing lung cancer is 2,000 percent higher for smoking males than non-smoking males, and 1,200 percent higher for smoking females than their non-smoking peers.

At present, between 35 and 40 percent of all new lung cancer cases are in current smokers. And, since the damage smoking does to the lungs is permanent and cumulative, former smokers, even those individuals who have not smoked in decades, are at greater risk of developing lung cancer than people who never smoked. According to Mark Kris, MD, of Sloan Kettering Memorial Hospital, New York City, "In the case of lung cancer, lifelong smoking allows genetic damage to accumulate to the point that cancer develops. Many feel that there are multiple steps from turning a normal cell into a malignant one. The

What is Lung Cancer?

exact number of steps, as well as the sequence of these steps, is not known, but these are the likely reasons lung cancer is so hard to figure out. People smoke for decades before developing the illness, and others often develop lung cancer decades after smoking has stopped."[13]

Approximately 50 percent of new lung cancer cases are in former smokers. Moreover, since the more an individual smokes the greater the damage to the lungs, the risk increases with the degree of exposure. For this reason, people who start smoking in their teens and continue to smoke as they age are at high risk. Lea, a seventy-eight-year-old former smoker and a lung cancer patient explains: "I am ... an ex-smoker. I smoked as a teen-ager and continued smoking for forty-some years. Of course, when I started smoking nobody knew the risks. I wish I had known when I was a teenager that smoking was not good for you and I wish that cigarettes were not so readily available to young people. I stopped smoking about ten years ago. Three years later, I had lung cancer."[14]

Individuals who start smoking later and/or stop smoking sooner, on the other hand, are less likely to develop or die of lung cancer than individuals who smoke all their lives. But they are still in more danger than people who never smoked. According to Dr. Kris, "There is no safe amount of cigarette smoking.

People who begin smoking cigarettes as teenagers have the highest risk of developing lung cancer later in their lifetimes.

Any degree of cigarette smoking can potentially cause lung cancer."[15]

Second Hand Smoke

Individuals do not have to be smokers, or even former smokers, to be harmed by tobacco smoke. Inhaling second hand smoke also causes lung cancer. It exposes the lungs to the same mix of dangerous chemicals as smoking. Although the extent of the exposure is not as significant as in smokers, long-term exposure to second hand smoke puts individuals at risk. This is why the Environmental Protection Agency lists environmental tobacco smoke in the most dangerous category of cancer causing agents. The agency estimates that three thousand non-smokers annually develop lung cancer due to exposure to second hand smoke. Indeed, non-smokers who live with smokers increase their risk of developing lung cancer by an estimated 24 percent compared to other non-smokers. Alice, a lung cancer survivor, explains that although she never smoked, both her parents did. She does not know what caused her to develop lung cancer, but she suspects it was her childhood exposure to secondhand smoke. "My parents did everything in their power to insure that I grew up healthy," she explains. "I was their only child, my mother almost died giving birth to me, and I'm sure that they would have given up their lives to protect me. They certainly would have given up smoking if they'd had any idea that it might one day harm me. But they had no idea."[16]

Other Harmful Substances

Exposure to radon, a radioactive gas that forms when uranium decays, is another substance linked to lung cancer. The gas, which is odorless and invisible, is found in the soil in varying quantities depending on the location. It can seep into buildings through gaps in the foundation and also through the plumbing. When it is inhaled, it releases radiation, which, over time, harms the lungs and causes cell mutation. The risk increases as radon levels rise.

What is Lung Cancer?

Childhood exposure to secondhand smoke may be the reason that some people who have never smoked develop lung cancer.

Twelve percent of all lung cancer deaths are associated with exposure to radon. A study, conducted in Iowa in 2000 and sponsored by the National Cancer Institute and the National Institute of Environmental Health Sciences, compared radon levels in the homes of 413 women diagnosed with lung cancer to the radon levels in the homes of 614 women without the disease. Both groups included smokers and non-smokers. The study found that the non-smokers who spent the equivalent of fifteen years exposed to radon were 50 percent more likely to develop lung cancer than other non-smokers. The subjects who smoked and were exposed to radon had a 1,200 percent increase in lung cancer risk compared to unexposed non-smokers. Smoking, the researchers say, makes the lungs more vulnerable to the effects of radon. Fortunately, buildings can be tested for radon and, if the gas is detected, it can be eliminated fairly easily.

About twelve thousand lung cancer cases each year are associated with radon. According to former U.S. Surgeon General Richard A. Carmona:

Air Pollution and Lung Cancer

Some scientists think there is a link between air pollution and lung cancer. A 2006 study conducted at the University of Texas Southwestern Medical Center, Dallas compared air pollution levels and lung cancer rates between 1995 and 2000 in 254 Texas counties. The study found that the incidence of lung cancer was highest in the counties that also had the highest levels of industrial air pollution, specifically metal particles such as zinc, copper, and chromium. The scientists theorized that inhaling the metal particles may make smokers more susceptible to lung cancer, and may be the cause of the rise in lung cancer among non-smokers. However, more studies are needed before this theory can be proven. Study author Dr. Yvonne Coyle explains: "It's disturbing that there might be something in the environment causing the problem. It could be these metals. We need to look further."

Quoted in Randy Dotinga, healthywomen.org, "Air Pollution Linked to Lung Cancer," September 18, 2006, www.healthywomen.org/resources/womenshealthinthenews/dbhealthnews/airpollution

Downtown Los Angeles shown cloaked in dirty air. Besides smoking, air pollution may be another cause of lung cancer.

What is Lung Cancer?

Indoor radon are associated with 12,000 lung cancer cases each year. Fortunately, there are many tests available to detect radon and the gas can be eliminated quite easily if found.

Indoor radon is the second-leading cause of lung cancer in the United States and breathing it over prolonged periods can present a significant health risk to families all over the county. It's important to know that this threat is completely preventable. Radon can be detected with a simple test and fixed through well-established venting techniques.[17]

Just as the radiation in radon causes lung cancer, so, too, does prolonged exposure to radiation from other sources. But radiation is not the only environmental toxin that can cause lung cancer. Almost any inhaled chemical can harm the lungs. Asbestos, in particular, poses a high risk. It is a mineral that was commonly used for insulation in buildings and naval vessels until the 1970s. It releases tiny fibers that damage the lungs when inhaled. An estimated 85 percent of all cases of mesothelioma, a rare type of lung cancer, are diagnosed in people who have been exposed to asbestos. Although asbestos use is limited today, workers in industries where asbestos is still used such as those who work in construction, shipyards, steel mills, oil refineries, and power plants are at risk.

Among asbestos workers, non-smokers have a five times greater chance of developing lung cancer than unexposed non-smokers. Those who smoke are more than 50 percent more likely to develop lung cancer than non-smokers who are not exposed to the mineral. Jim, a lung cancer patient, describes what happened to him:

> I was a heavy smoker for over twenty years. During that time I never smoked less than a pack a day; sometimes it was two. Most of my adult life I worked in construction and was therefore exposed to things like wallboard dust, drywall dust, gypsum, wood resins, pressure-treated

Top Ten Cancers for Men and Women In 2003

Type of Cancer	Number of Cases Per 100,000
Prostate	150
Female Breast	119
Lung	87
Colorectal	60
Uterine	23
Bladder	37
Non-Hodgkin Lymphoma	22
Skin	21
Kidney	19
Ovary	13

Source: Centers for Disease Control and Prevention. Available online at: http://apps.nccd.cdc.gov/uscs/Table.aspx?Group=3f&Year=2003&Display=n.

lumber, paint fumes, and ... asbestos too. I have a picture in my mind of a day when I was cutting bricks. Red dust was coming up. But I wasn't wearing a gas mask. It would have been inconvenient because I had a cigarette hanging out of my mouth. I couldn't say, "How could this possibly happen?"[18]

Still, the diagnosis was a shock.

Hard Hit Groups

Prolonged exposure to inhaled carcinogens raises everyone's chance of developing lung cancer. African Americans, however, are more likely to develop and die of lung cancer than any other ethnic group. According to the American Lung Association, the lung cancer incidence rate in African American males is 50 percent higher than that of their Caucasian counterparts. This is despite the fact that African American men are less likely to smoke than Caucasian men. Those who do, however, are more likely to develop lung cancer than Caucasian male smokers. The same holds true for African American females. Although they smoke less than Caucasian women, they develop lung cancer at the same rate.

An African American's ability to survive lung cancer is also worse. The group's five-year survival rate is about 13 percent compared to 15 percent for Caucasians. Scientists do not know why African Americans are hit so hard. It may be that their bodies process tobacco and other carcinogens differently than people of other ethnicities.

Gender

Gender also plays a role in who gets lung cancer. The disease affects both men and women, and more men have lung cancer than women. Yet women who smoke or have smoked are more likely to develop lung cancer than men with the same history, particularly at lower levels of exposure to cigarettes. It is unclear

Light Cigarettes, Cigars, and Lung Cancer

Light cigarettes contain less tar, a carcinogen, than regular cigarettes. Consequently, many smokers think that smoking light cigarettes cuts their risk of developing lung cancer. A 2004 study by the Massachusetts Institute of Technology in Boston found that this was not so. People who smoke light cigarettes have the same risk of dying of lung cancer as other filtered cigarette smokers. The study tracked one million smokers for six years, comparing the type of cigarettes they smoked with lung cancer deaths. Smokers who smoked light cigarettes and those who smoked regular filtered cigarettes were at equal risk. Those who smoked non-filtered cigarettes were at the highest risk. This is because filters block the biggest chemical particles from reaching the lungs.

Some cigar smokers, too, think that smoking cigars is safe. Because most cigar smokers do not inhale, they are at lower risk of developing and dying of lung cancer than cigarette smokers. But they are at higher risk than non-smokers. In addition, cigar smoking causes mouth, tongue, lips, throat, and esophagus cancer.

Scientific studies have proven that light cigarettes, like those pictured here, do not reduce the risk of developing lung cancer.

why this occurs. Scientists theorize that smoking causes greater damage to a woman's signaling genes than it does to a man's.

An eight-year study beginning in 1999, sponsored by the Weill Medical College in New York City, compared lung cancer rates in 9,427 men and 7,498 women. All of the subjects were current or former smokers. Although there were 1,929 more male subjects than female, over the course of the study 156 women developed lung cancer as compared to 113 men. That amounts to about 20 percent of the females and 12 percent of the males, a significant difference.

Journalist Lauren Terrazano, who died of lung cancer on May 15, 2007, had this to say about lung cancer's impact on women:

> Lung cancer rates in women continue to rise. I know this, because I am one of those so-called statistics, though I am much more than that. The fact is, lung cancer is the No. 1 cancer killer of women, whose lifetime risk of developing it is one in seventeen... I smoked off and on for about five years, not really the profile of the typical smoker who developed the disease as a result of her bad habit.[19]

Nonsmoking women, too, are at greater risk of developing lung cancer than nonsmoking men. They are two to three times more likely to develop the disease than their male counterparts. In the United States, about ten percent of all lung cancer cases are diagnosed in nonsmokers. This translates to an estimated twenty to twenty-six thousand people annually. Eighty percent are women. And, in other countries non-smoking women are hit even harder. For example, thirty-three percent of all lung cancer cases in Singapore occur in nonsmokers, most of whom are female. Once again, scientists do not understand why this occurs. Some speculate that women's lungs are more susceptible to damage caused by second-hand smoke and other environmental toxins than those of men.

Writer and former spokeswoman for the Lung Cancer Alliance Sandy Phillips Britt was one of these unfortunate women. In 2007, she wrote:

Two and a half years ago when I was 46, I was diagnosed with the most advanced stage of lung cancer. I've never smoked a day in my life. In fact, I hate smoking almost to a fanatical degree.... Nonsmoking women are a faster growing population of lung cancer victims than anyone realizes. I did everything you're supposed to do to ward off disease and death. I ate right, exercised, got plenty of sleep, wore sunscreen, got yearly mammograms, locked my car doors and always wore my seat belt.[20]

Although healthy living is a person's best defense against any disease, including lung cancer, even people like Britt can develop lung cancer. In most cases, smoking and exposure to certain carcinogens cause the disease to develop, but not always.

CHAPTER TWO

Symptoms and Diagnosis

In its early stages lung cancer does not usually produce symptoms. Consequently, over 50 percent of lung cancer cases are not diagnosed until the disease is advanced. When symptoms do arise, they are frequently mistaken for other, less serious, illnesses. To ascertain that the problem is indeed lung cancer, a variety of diagnostic tools are used. Once the presence of lung cancer is established, the particular type and stage of the cancer must be identified before treatment can begin.

Few Symptoms

People with lung cancer rarely complain of symptoms in the early stage of the disease. The lungs' large size and the fact that the organ does not contain nerve endings makes it possible for a tumor to grow in or on the lungs without causing any pain. Nor do most people with lung cancer usually experience breathing problems early on. The lungs are filled with a network of airways that provide individuals with more breathing capacity than they ordinarily require. So even if a small tumor develops in an airway, breathing will not be an issue until the tumor enlarges and blocks the airway.

Because lung cancer does not produce clear symptoms until the disease advances, most people with lung cancer do not seek medical attention until the cancer has metastasized. This is the main reason five-year survival rates are so poor. "Ordinarily," explains authors Claudia I. Henschke, Peggy McCarthy, and Sarah Wernick, "a lung cancer tumor isn't discovered until it causes symptoms. By then the tumor usually is about the size of a small orange and the cancer probably has already spread."[21]

That is what happened to Sandy Phillips Britt, who had lung cancer for three years before it was detected:

> You might wonder: How could I go more than three years with lung cancer and not know it? It is because I had absolutely no symptoms until I started coughing in July 2004. One reason lung cancer kills so many people is that symptoms don't appear until it is too late.[22]

When lung cancer is detected in its early stages, it is often by accident. It may be discovered during a routine physical exam if a chest x-ray is administered. That is what happened to Cindy Bass. She remembers: "My lung cancer was discovered ... during a routine examination with my long-term primary care physician. For five years, as part of my annual check-up, I had been receiving a chest x-ray. But this time, my doctor saw something peculiar .... lung cancer."[23]

Or it is sometimes detected when patients seek medical help for other health issues, which is what happened to Anita Johnson, a lung cancer survivor. She explains:

> I was visiting my daughter in Florida when I was involved in a car accident. The car was totaled and I was taken to the hospital. A chest x-ray showed a scar on my lung. "Oh sure, I know about that," I said. "I had pneumonia when I was young. That scar's been there since I was 26." The doctor insisted on doing a CAT scan [a more detailed imaging test] ... and sure enough, this thing on my lung was malignant. I'm very fortunate to have been diagnosed at stage 1A [a very early stage] ... Had I not had that accident and waited until I had symptoms, things could have turned out differently.[24]

Symptoms and Diagnosis

Confusing Symptoms

As the disease advances, symptoms start to arise. For the most part, the symptoms depend on where the tumor is located. For instance, if the tumor is located in the airways, it can reduce the supply of oxygen to the blood as it enlarges, causing fatigue, wheezing, and shortness of breath. Large tumors in the airways can also cause patients to develop a chronic cough, which was Tammy's only symptom. She recalls: "I had had a cough for about a year, and my son used to tease me. He used to say, 'Mom have you thought of getting that cough checked on?' And I would just laugh because the cough had become such a part of me."[25]

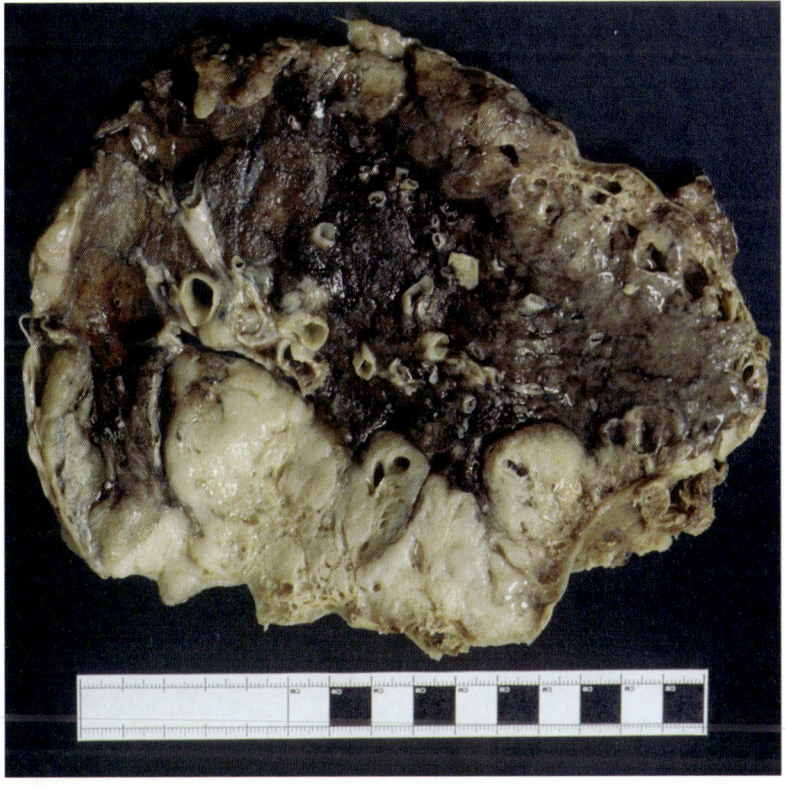

A piece of a human lung containing a cancer tumor (white) on the bottom. In some cases lung cancer is symptomless until the tumor becomes too large for the patient to recover.

If the tumor presses on a blood vessel, the patient may cough up blood and/or mucus. A tumor that touches the larynx or voice box leads to hoarseness. Television news anchor Peter Jennings, who died of lung cancer, reported hoarseness as his primary symptom.

Trouble swallowing is another symptom. It develops if the tumor compresses the esophagus, the tube that leads from the mouth to the stomach. Some individuals also develop pain in their neck, shoulders, or chest. This happens if the tumor makes contact with nerves in these areas. Once the tumor metastasizes, other symptoms appear. These include general cancer symptoms such as weight loss, a low-grade fever, loss of appetite, and weakness, as well as symptoms that relate to the part of the body where the tumor has lodged. For example, if the cancer spreads to the brain, headaches are common.

What makes diagnosing lung cancer tricky is that these symptoms rarely cluster together, nor are they specific to lung cancer. Often, they are attributed to less serious conditions such as fatigue, stress, a muscle or bone injury, acid reflux, or a respiratory infection like a cold, sinus infection, the flu, bronchitis, or pneumonia.

Before she was diagnosed with lung cancer, Kathleen's symptoms confused her doctors for months. She explains:

> Last summer in July, my left shoulder started hurting. When it still hurt after a couple of weeks, I went to my doctor. He recommended ibuprofen and several exercises. When it still hurt a month later, he recommended physical therapy. A month later, I saw an orthopedic surgeon [a doctor who specializes in bones and muscles], who said I did not need surgery, but just wait it out: 'That's why they call it a pain in the neck, because it takes a long time to heal.'...
>
> Then came the holidays... Then back to the doctor in February. He recommended either an MRI [a medical device that takes pictures of soft tissue], a different

orthopedic doctor, or more physical therapy. I didn't want to spend the money on any of them, but I was considering the options when I started coughing up a little blood.... [A week later] I came down with a fever and started feeling sick. The next day I went to the doctor. The regular doctor was out, but the associate diagnosed me with a sinus infection, even though I did not have sinus pain. She said she could see yellow junk in my sinuses, and the coughing of blood would be consistent with a sinus infection—drainage and coughing up. She gave me an antibiotic. My activity level went down and the coughing of blood stopped for several days; as I got more active, it resumed... [About a week later] I finally went for a chest x-ray, where this tennis ball tumor showed up. That's what had been causing the pain.[26]

Kathleen's experience is not unusual. Because lung cancer symptoms are easily confused with other conditions, the disease is frequently misdiagnosed. In fact, most people are treated for other conditions first. It is only when symptoms fail to resolve, that lung cancer is suspected. According to Henschke, McCarthy, and Wernick, "Misdiagnosis is a common problem with lung cancer—and it can make the difference between life and death. Many people ... describe repeated medical visits, sometimes over many weeks or months before the true cause of their problem is identified."[27]

Imaging Tests

When treatment for other illnesses fail imaging tests, which check for abnormalities in the lungs, are administered. Usually the first step is a chest x-ray, which uses a small amount of radiation to take a black and white, two-dimensional picture of the chest cavity. Irregularities on the lungs appear as gray or white spots on the picture. One lung cancer survivor recalls:

I went into the regular doctor's office and had a chest x-ray. It showed the tumor on the lung. They said from the beginning that it was a tumor, but not that it was necessarily cancer. It was good-sized, a little bigger than a golf ball. Even I could see it plainly on the x-ray.[28]

Tumors about the size of a grape or larger can be detected on an x-ray, but the grainy quality and lack of detail of an x-ray image makes it difficult to detect smaller tumors, or the extent or exact site of a large tumor. Therefore, in order to gain more information about a tumor, or if the x-ray is negative but the patient's symptoms are suspicious, a computer axial tomography scan (CT or CAT scan) is administered. It takes a series of high resolution x-rays that come up on a computer monitor, forming a detailed, three-dimensional cross-section of the lungs. CT scans are so accurate that they can detect a tumor as small as a grain of rice. The scan can also pinpoint the exact location and size of a tumor. And by imaging other organs such as the brain or abdomen, a CT scan can determine whether the cancer has spread to these sites.

During a CT scan, patients lie on a moving table that passes through an imaging machine shaped like a large ring. The machine takes pictures at different angles of the patient's lungs. Often the patient is injected with a harmless radioactive dye before the scan. It increases the contrast between different tissues.

The scan takes about ten minutes and is painless. Patients are asked to hold their breath for short periods during the scan, but not through its entirety. Author and physician Henschke, describes the scan she administered to her patient, Michael:

> Michael lay down on the scanning table. He took a deep breath and held it. Silently, the table glided through the scanning doughnut—a vertical ring about as big as a tractor tire. Before he exhaled, the device had already created detailed images of his lungs…When I bring up the images of his lungs on my computer screen, I see something I don't want to see, The large oval on the right—his left lung—is black as it's supposed to be. But on the bottom of the left oval is an ominous irregularly shaped shadow of gray.[29]

Symptoms and Diagnosis

A patient undergoing a computer axial tomography, or CT scan, on the lungs. The CT scan is an effective tool for diagnosing lung cancer.

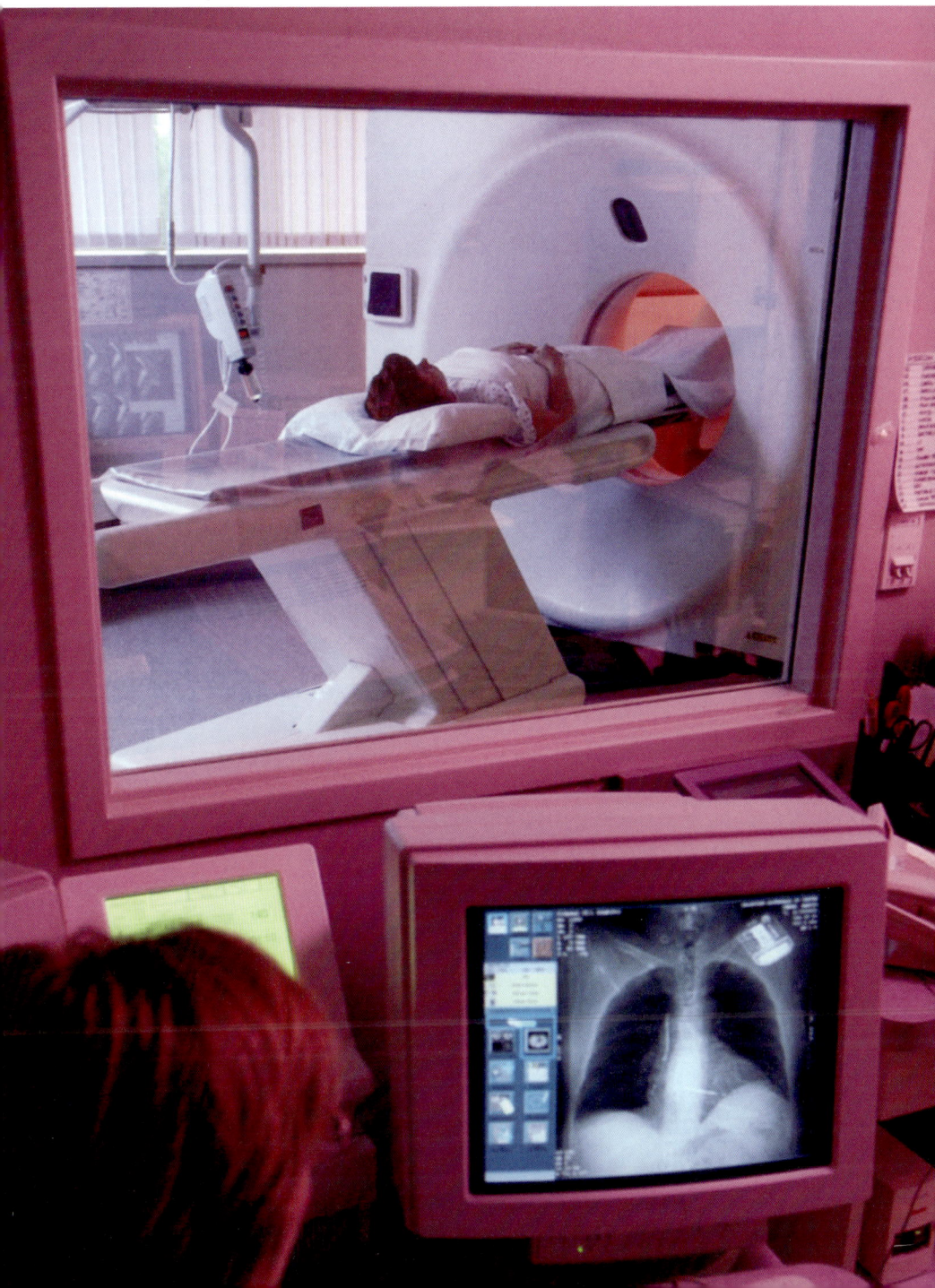

The Lung Cancer Team

People with lung cancer depend on a team of healthcare professionals for diagnosis and treatment. First, there is the patient's family doctor. He or she is usually the first person individuals consult with when they have health problems. A pulmonologist, a doctor who specializes in diagnosing and treating diseases of the lungs, is the professional most likely to take a lung biopsy, and a pathologist, a physician who examines and evaluates cells, analyzes tissue from the biopsy.

Once the pathologist establishes that the patient has lung cancer, an oncologist, a doctor who specializes in cancer, joins the team. Other healthcare professionals are also likely to be a part of the patient's care. There are oncology nurses who specialize in caring for cancer patients, thoracic surgeons who perform lung surgery, radiation oncologists who administer radiation therapy, social workers who counsel patients and locate special services patients may need, psychiatrists who help patients deal with emotional issues, and rehabilitation specialists like physical and respiratory therapists who help patients increase their physical strength and their breathing capacity.

Analyzing Cells

The discovery of a suspicious mass on an x-ray or CT scan does not conclusively prove that the culprit is cancer. The mass can be a benign tumor, fluid caused by pneumonia, a cyst, or scar tissue. The only way to determine if it is indeed lung cancer is via a biopsy. That is a procedure in which lung tissue is removed and sent to a laboratory, where a specialized doctor known as a pathologist studies the sample under a microscope in order to determine whether the cells are normal or cancerous.

Symptoms and Diagnosis

Removing the cells can be accomplished in a number of ways, including a bronchoscopy. During this procedure, the patient's throat and nostrils are sprayed with a numbing gel. Then a pulmonolgist, a doctor who specializes in diseases of the lungs, inserts a long thin tube about ½ inch wide (0.13 cm) and 2 feet long (0.61 m) called a bronchoscope through the patient's nose into the windpipe and down to the lungs. The bronchoscope has two fiber optic devices inside it. One transmits light. The other receives images that are displayed on a computer monitor. This allows the doctor to see into the airways and locate the tumor. Once the tumor's location is established a biopsy device, which may be a needle, forceps, or a tiny brush, is inserted into the bronchoscope. All these devices remove tissue from the tumor as well as from nearby lymph nodes in order to check if the cancer has spread. However, if the tumor is deep in the lungs or on the outer edges of

A female patient undergoing bronchoscope. This procedure is used to remove cells in the lungs so that they can be analyzed to determine if they are cancerous or not.

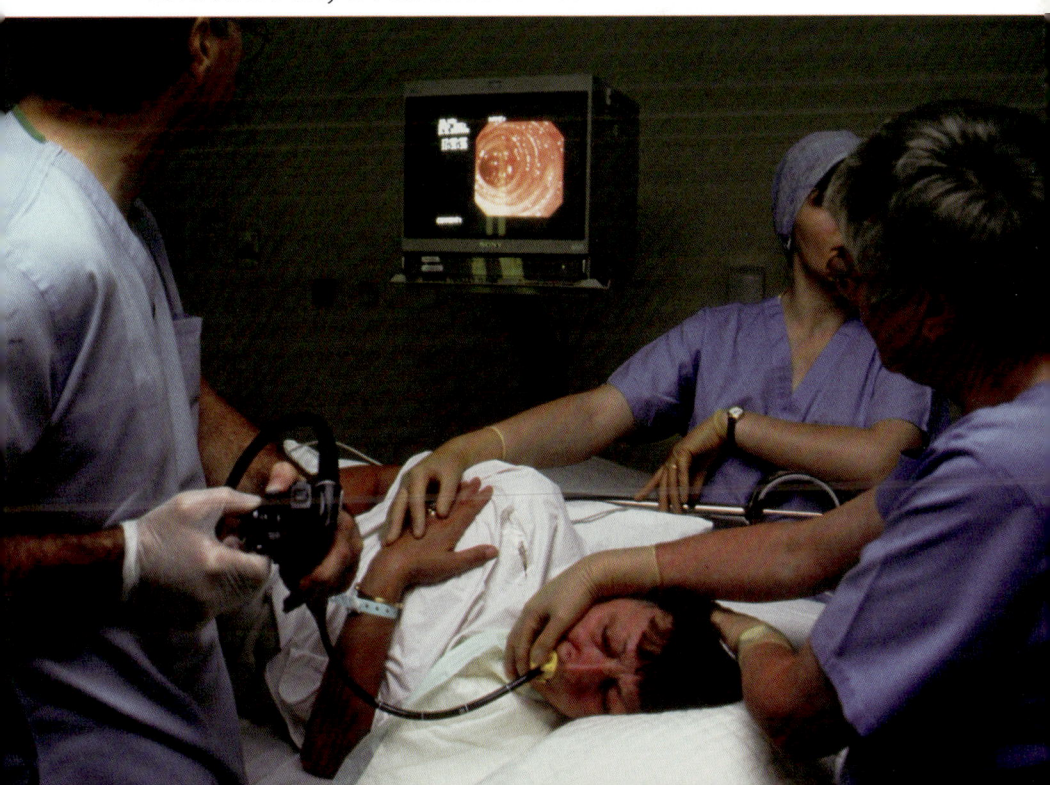

the lungs, the bronchoscope cannot reach it or even see it. So although a bronchoscopy is a valuable tool, it is not always effective in diagnosing all cases of lung cancer. For instance, it was ineffective in detecting lung cancer survivor, Francine's tumor. She recalls: "The test was done and came back clean which meant negative. From the beginning, Dr. Hutter [Francine's physician] had explained to me that the test may not show anything if she took a sample from a location that wasn't malignant."[30]

When a bronchoscopy is ineffective, a needle biopsy is another option. It is a procedure in which a thin needle with a cutting tip or a vacuum-assisted device is inserted into the chest wall in order to withdraw tumor tissue. To ensure the needle is positioned correctly, the procedure is usually performed in conjunction with a CT scan. This allows the doctor to precisely target the tumor. If the patient's symptoms suggest that the cancer has spread to other organs, a needle biopsy of the liver or spine may also be administered. To reduce any discomfort during the procedure, patients are given a general anesthetic which does not put them to sleep, but simply numbs the area in which the needle is inserted. William, a lung cancer survivor describes his experience:

> I was ushered into still another CT facility. I was told that long needles would be inserted into my chest cavity from different angles to, hopefully, obtain tissues samples from the spot... I laid back on a hard scanning table and watched as they pressed the long needles into my chest. The procedure seemed to go on forever.... but fortunately ... they thought they might have gotten a usable sample.[31]

Sometimes neither a needle nor a bronchoscope can reach a tumor. In this case, surgery is the best way to retrieve tissue samples. There are two different procedures that may be performed. Both are administered in a hospital, where patients are sedated.

The first procedure, called mediastinoscopy, looks at and gathers tissue samples from the mediastinum, the middle or space between the lungs. The lymph nodes, located here, are usually the first place lung cancer spreads. The second procedure, known as a video assisted thorascopy (VATS), examines and harvests tissue from the lining of the chest and the periphery of the lungs. In both procedures a scope, similar to a bronchoscope, is inserted into the patient through an incision made either in the patient's breastbone or side. A very small video camera attached to the scope allows the doctor to view the lungs on a computer monitor. The physician uses these images to guide instruments that remove suspicious tissue samples.

Distinguishing the Type and Stage of Cancer

Harvested tissues are sent to a laboratory, where besides establishing whether cancer is indeed present, the type and stage of lung cancer is determined. These factors are vital in prescribing the most effective treatment.

There are two basic types of lung cancer: small cell lung cancer (SCLC), and non-small cell lung cancer (NSCLC), which are distinguished by their appearance under a microscope. Approximately 20 to 25 percent of all lung cancer cases are small cell lung cancer. This type of lung cancer is almost always linked to smoking. It is usually more aggressive than non-small cell cancer, with a doubling time of about thirty days. Because it grows and spreads so rapidly, symptoms appear sooner. It usually begins in the airways rather than on the surface of the lungs.

Non-small cell cancer is the most common type of the disease. There are three different forms of NSCLC: adenocarcinoma, squamous cell carcinoma, and large cell carcinoma. Though smoking is the primary cause of all forms of NSCLC, it also affects non-smokers. NSCLC usually begins in the alveoli (another name for the air sacs in the lungs), in the airways, or in the bronchial tubes in the center of the lungs.

A chest x-ray showing stage III lung cancer. This stage of cancer has not yet metastasized to other organs of the body.

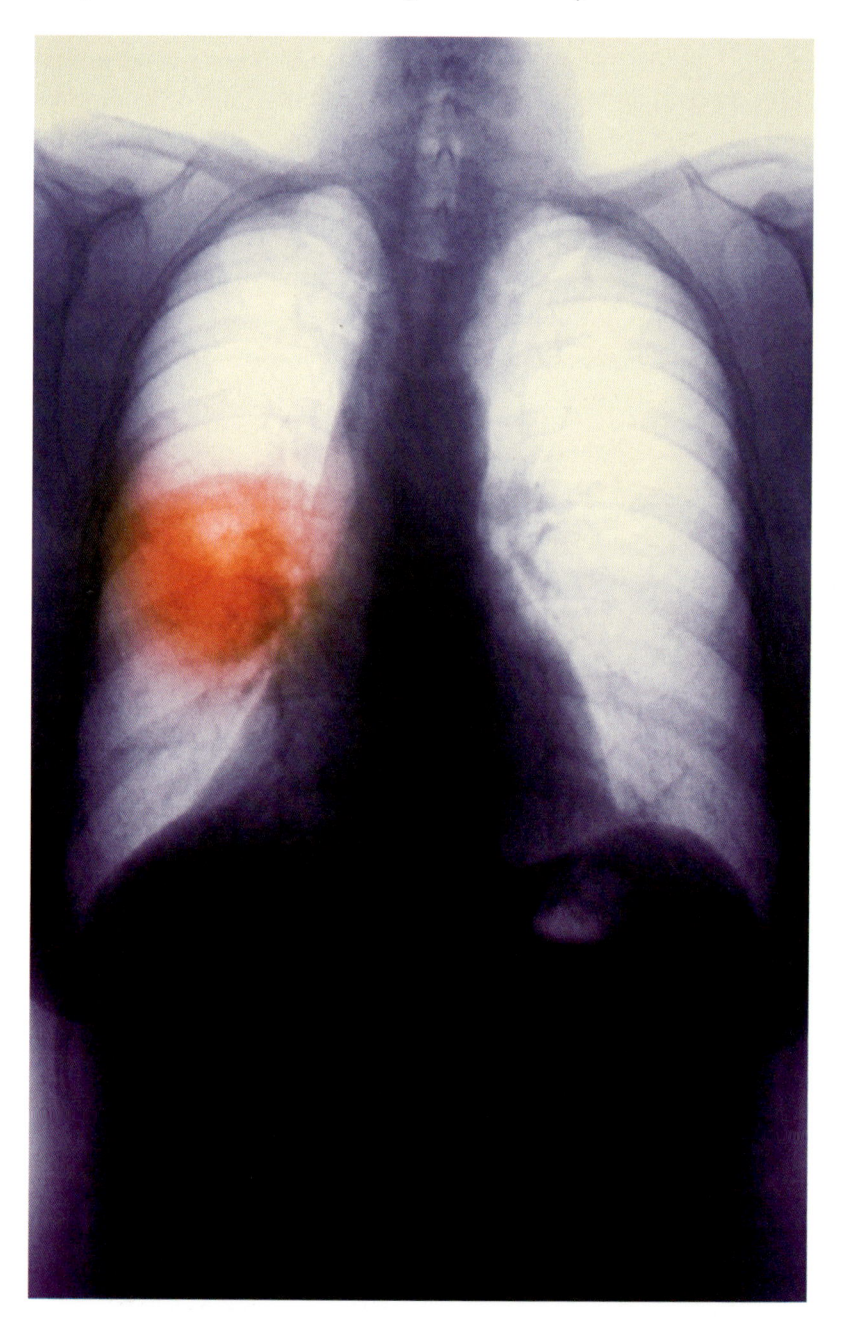

Symptoms and Diagnosis

Once the type of lung cancer is established the pathologist identifies the cancer stage: the size and location of the tumor, whether it has spread, and if so, how far from the lungs. Examining cells taken from different parts of the lungs and the lymph nodes lets the pathologist make this assessment. Unlike most cancers, which are divided into four stages, SCLC is divided into only two stages because it spreads so rapidly: limited, which means the cancer is present in only one lung and/or nearby lymph nodes, or extensive, meaning the cancer has spread into both lungs and/or other organs. All forms of NSCLC, on the other hand, are divided into four stages, stage I, II, III, or IV. In stage I, the tumor is small and is confined to the lungs. Stage II means the cancer has spread to nearby lymph nodes, or the tumor touches the chest wall without affecting the lymph nodes. In stage III, the cancer has advanced into lymph nodes on either side of the chest, or into the chest area, but has not metastasized to distant organs. When cancer cells have spread to distant organs like the brain or liver, the disease has reached stage IV.

Making a Prognosis

Once the type and stage of cancer are established, the doctor uses this information to make a prognosis. This is an estimate of how likely the patient is to be cured, or what the patient's long-term survival chances are. It is based on statistics on how well other patients with the same type and stage of lung cancer fared. In general, the prognosis for SCLC is worse than for NSCLC, and the higher the stage of cancer, the poorer the prognosis.

While early stage NSCLC has a 70 percent cure rate, by stage III or IV the five-year survival rates falls to anywhere from 5 to 15 percent. Unfortunately, more than 50 percent of NSCLC cases are diagnosed at stage III or IV. However, a prognosis is only a prediction and each individual is different. Larry, a lung cancer survivor, puts it this way:

> Statistics give some people a reference point... There are many variables when talking about lung cancer that no

one statistic can be used with any degree of accuracy... Five years ago, I was diagnosed with limited stage small cell lung cancer located in the right upper lobe. The doctor making the initial diagnosis told me to "go home and get your affairs in order," and gave me a one in twelve chance of survival... I don't believe in statistics.[32]

Indeed, because lung cancer does not usually produce symptoms early on, and even when symptoms do appear, they are easily confused with those of other ailments, many individuals are not diagnosed until the disease has advanced. They therefore face a poor prognosis. A prognosis, however, is an inexact prediction. Once a diagnosis is made, no matter the prognosis, steps can be taken to increase an individual's chance of survival.

CHAPTER THREE

Treatment

Once a diagnosis is made, lung cancer treatment begins. Each patient's treatment plan depends on the type and stage of the disease. Treatments include surgery, radiation, and chemotherapy. Unfortunately, lung cancer treatment can cause a number of unpleasant side effects. To better cope with these side effects, some patients turn to non-traditional complementary treatments.

Surgical Treatment

Surgery is used as a first-line treatment in cases of stage I and II and sometimes stage III NSCLC. It involves the surgical removal of cancer cells and surrounding tissue from the body. In most cases of SCLC, and stage IV NSCLC, the cancer is too widespread for surgical removal. Or it infects more of the lung than can be surgically removed without affecting the patient's ability to breath, general health, or quality of life.

When surgery is an option, a thoracic surgeon, a doctor who specializes in surgery of the lungs, performs it. If the surgery involves the removal of a single small tumor, video-assisted thoracoscopic surgery is performed. It is done just like a video-assisted thoracoscopy and utilizes the same equipment. However, rather than removing a tissue sample, the whole tumor is removed. This form of surgery is not very invasive, and therefore has a short recovery period. But the delicate equipment and the small incision that characterize this procedure do not allow the removal of large or multiple tumors.

A thoracic surgeon performing surgery to remove a tumor from a cancer patient's lungs.

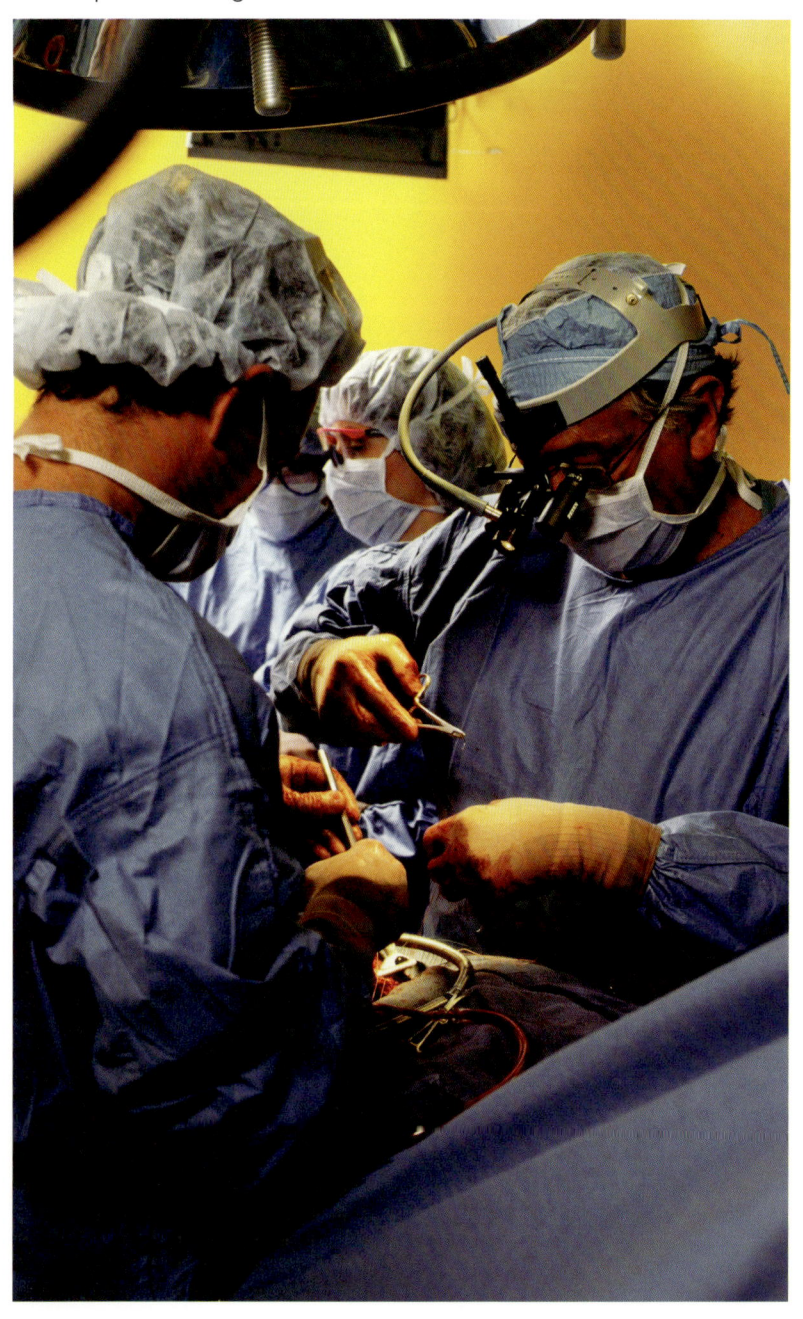

Treatment

For those patients with large or multiple tumors other surgical procedures are needed. A lobectomy is among the most common. The lungs contain five lobes or sections, three in the right lung, and two in the left. A lobectomy involves the removal of the tumor and the lobe in which the tumor is situated, as well as nearby lymph nodes and blood vessels. This helps keep stray cancer cells from spreading to distant organs.

Sometimes more than one lobe must be removed. If the tumor is in the airways, or it involves all the lobes on one side, a pneumonectomy is called for. In this procedure, the whole lung plus adjacent lymph nodes and blood vessels are removed. Fortunately, most people can live with one lung.

During both surgeries patients are connected to an IV tube through which sedating medication is administered. Once the patient is asleep, a breathing tube is inserted through the patient's mouth into their lungs. Then the surgeon makes an incision between the patient's ribs. It extends from under the arms to the side and back and is about 8 inches (20.32 centimeters) in length. Next, in order to gain access to the lungs, the surgeon cuts into the patient's chest muscles and cracks some of the patient's ribs in order to separate them. One or more tubes are inserted into the chest through the patient's side. These drains air and fluid from the lungs during the surgery.

Now the patient is ready for the surgeon to carefully remove the tumor or tumors, surrounding tissue, adjacent blood vessels, and lymph nodes. The surgeon then staples or sews the incision closed, leaving the air tube in place. It is common for air from lung tissue to leak into the chest cavity after lung cancer surgery. If too much air leaks out, external pressure causes the lungs to collapse. The air tube, which is removed once all danger has passed, keeps this from occurring.

Post-surgery, patients usually stay in the hospital from four to ten days. At first they are connected to special machines that check their vital functions, and to an IV that delivers antibiotics and pain medication. Some individuals require assistance breathing. A respirator, a machine attached to a tube placed down the patient's windpipe, does this by causing the patient's lungs to inflate and deflate automatically. And because, as with all surgeries, there is a risk of infection and blood clots, patients are monitored for any sign of illness. Since exercise helps prevent blood clots and a form of pneumonia that is linked to lying flat for long periods, nurses encourage and help recovering individuals to get out of bed. While a respiratory therapist, a healthcare professional who evaluates, cares for, and treats patients with respiratory problems, provides the patient with rehabilitative breathing exercises to strengthen the remaining lung tissue. A man who had a lung removed recalls his experience: "In the hospital, I didn't feel like doing much. Getting out of bed and walking, taking a shower, took about three or four days… But I did have a lot of breathing therapy—lung capacity, how much you could breathe, inhale antibiotics, respiratory therapy—trying to increase capacity."[33]

Radiation Therapy

In some cases, lung cancer surgery removes all traces of cancer and no further treatment is needed. Natalie's was one of these cases. She reports:

> On the day of my surgery, before the July heat began to broil the city, Dr. Scott opened my chest and removed my whole left lung…The morning after the surgery, my doctor pulled a chair to the side of my bed. "The operation was a success," he said… I wake up these days glad to be alive.[34]

But in more than half of lung cancer cases radiation therapy is required. It may be administered before surgery to shrink a large tumor, after surgery to combat the possibility that microscopic cancer cells may still remain in the lungs, or in combination with chemotherapy as a way to slow down the progress of advanced lung cancer when surgery is not viable.

Radiation therapy uses x-rays and other forms of radiation, such as gamma rays, to change the structure of cancer cells so

Treatment

that they can no longer divide. During radiation therapy a beam of radiation is directed at the part of the lungs where the tumor is located. Since radiation also damages normal cells, every effort is made to ensure that the beam is precisely focused so that only the infected area is treated. With this in mind, before treatment begins, a doctor known as a radiation oncologist positions the patient on a treatment bed, then measures the correct angles to aim the radiation beams. The patient's skin is marked with ink to identify the treatment field or fields, which, depending on how far the cancer has spread, may be one or multiple. At the same time shields, used to keep the beam away from healthy organs near the treatment field, are fitted. This process is known as a simulation.

A lung cancer patient undergoing radiation therapy. This treatment is used to shrink large cancer tumors or to kill microscopic cancer cells that may still be in the body after surgery.

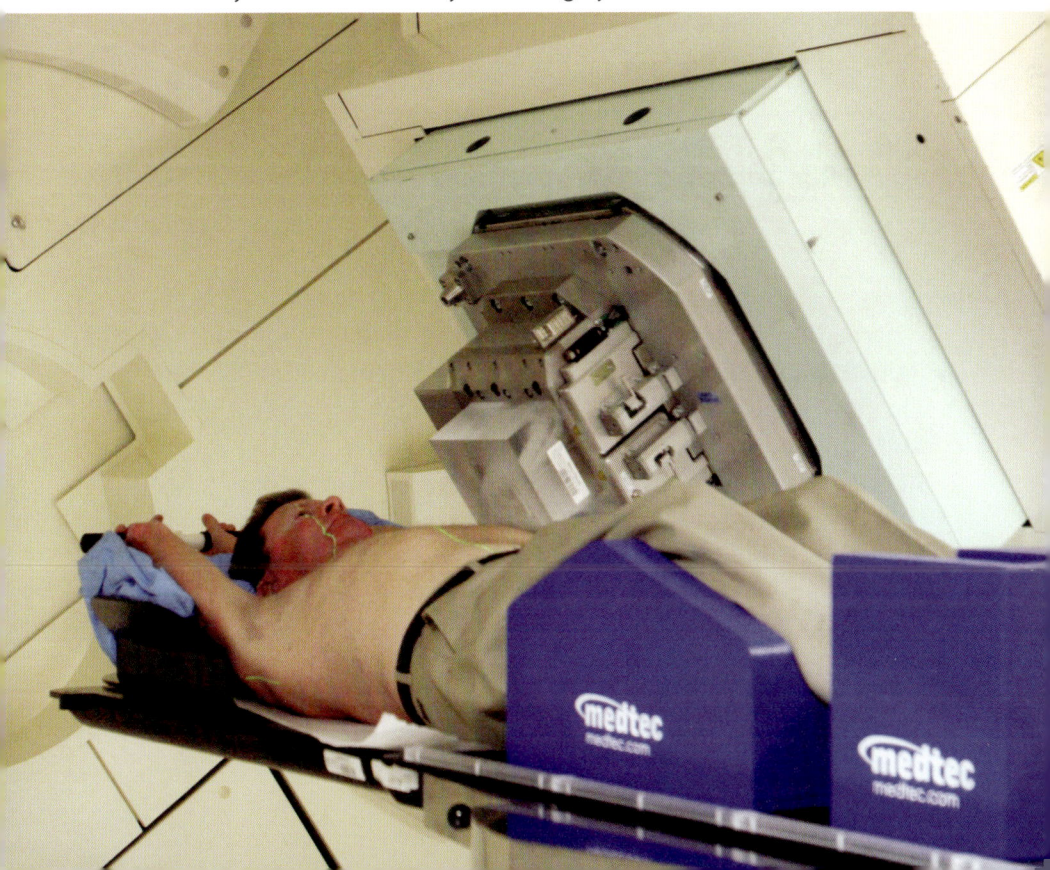

What are Clinical Trials?

Taking part in a clinical trial is one way some people with advanced lung cancer try to control the disease. Clinical trials are research studies with human subjects. Hospitals, research institutions, and drug manufacturers sponsor most clinical trials.

Some clinical trials test the effectiveness of new medications. Other trials analyze how well new combinations of medicines, new doses of proven medicines, or new ways to administer medication help combat lung cancer.

Trials are divided into three phases. Phase I aims to determine whether a particular treatment is safe for humans. Phase II focuses on establishing the treatment's effectiveness, while phase III compares the treatment's effectiveness to proven treatments.

Patients are given some form of treatment in all three phases. In phases I and II, all subjects receive the test treatment. In phase III, a control group is administered a proven treatment, while the other subjects are administered the test treatment.

Radiation therapy itself is painless. It is usually administered daily in ten to thirty minute sessions for about six weeks. During these sessions patients lie on a bed similar to an examining table inside a room with thick lead-clad walls, which prevent radiation from escaping. Above the bed is a machine much like an x-ray machine. While the patient lies still, the machine moves around the bed delivering radiation to the treatment field.

Chemotherapy

As with radiation, chemotherapy may be administered before surgery, to shrink a tumor so as to make it operable, or after, to destroy any cancer cells that might have been left behind. When surgery is not an option, chemotherapy is the most common lung cancer treatment. It may be combined with radiation or administered alone. The goal is to destroy cancer cells, thus curing the disease. However, in some cases the cancer may be too widespread to cure. Chemotherapy is then used as a palliative treatment—a treatment aimed at slowing tumor growth, thereby increasing survival time. University of California, professor Thierry Jahan, MD, explains:

> When I started out, anybody with advanced lung cancer was given a pat on the back and a "good luck." We went from essentially no treatment options to not only realizing treatments are effective, but we're able to push back the clock for a lot of people. It's not unusual to see people live, and live well, for three or five years.[35]

A cancer patient watches television as she undergoes chemotherapy, a procedure that uses powerful drugs to prevent the cancer cells from dividing and spreading throughout the body.

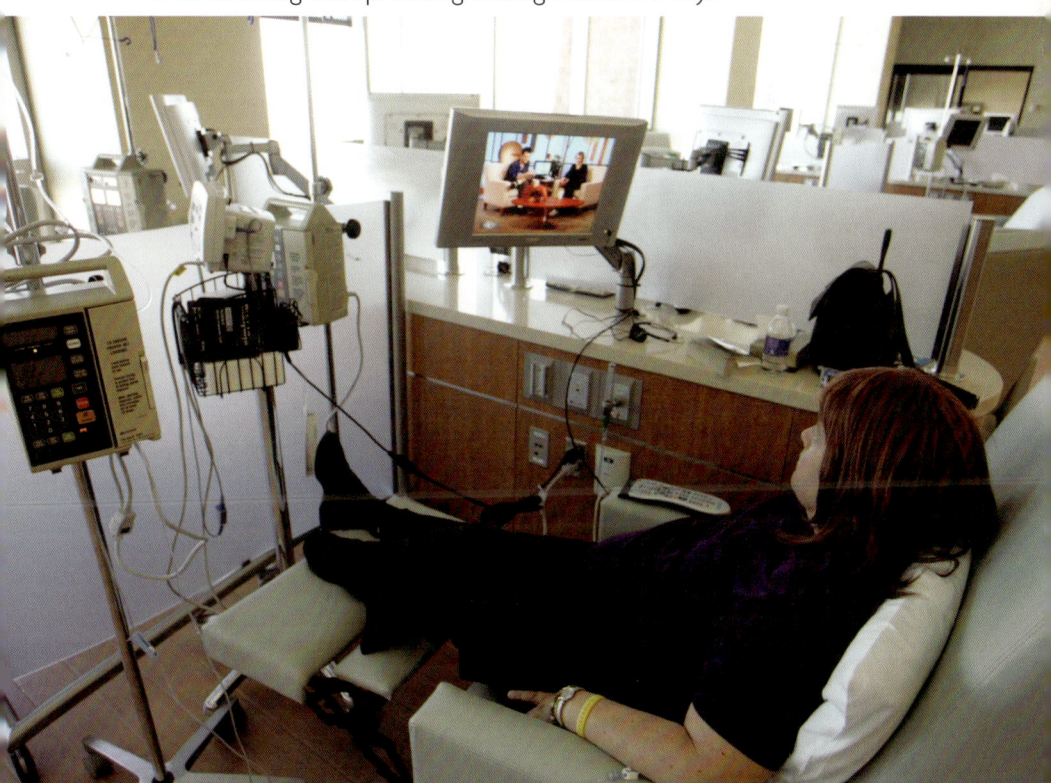

Chemotherapy for lung cancer uses a mix of powerful drugs that prevent both healthy and malignant cells from dividing. Since cancer cells divide rapidly, they are especially vulnerable to chemotherapy. Because chemotherapy is administered intravenously, requiring patients to endure multiple needle sticks during the course of the therapy, many patients are fitted with a port or a catheter before chemotherapy starts. A catheter is a thin tube, one end of which is inserted into a vein near the heart. The other end sticks out of the patient's chest. A port has an identical tube inserted into the same vein at one end. The other end is attached to a plastic disk that is implanted into the patient's chest. The port has a small hole that sticks out of the skin. Medication is administered through the catheter tube or the port hole, which allows patients to avoid frequent needle sticks. Donna, a lung cancer survivor, explains: "My veins are very deep and very small, and they were difficult to find for chemotherapy. I was having a lot of anxiety about the needles. My doctor suggested a port in my chest. With the port, the nurses could get a sure hit every time."[36]

Generally, chemotherapy is administered in cycles with a rest period in between. For example, six cycles of chemotherapy may be administered once a week for a period of three weeks, followed by a three-week break. The break allows normal cells damaged by chemotherapy drugs to recover. The number of cycles, duration of the cycles, number and length of each session, and the mix of drugs administered depends on the patient, and is based on the stage and type of lung cancer. "Mine was 5 days on, 21 days off," Larry, who credits chemotherapy with his survival, explains: "The infusions started at 9 AM and I was done and home usually by 12:30. Just in time to watch my cooking shows…. Would I do it again if I had to? You bet! In a heartbeat!"[37]

Treatments usually take place in a special hospital suite equipped with recliner chairs on which a number of patients relax as intravenous bags drip medicine into their bodies. Most rooms are outfitted with televisions and reading material. Patients may sleep, listen to music, or visit with each other,

Treatment

or with friends and family members that accompany them. Journalist and lung cancer patient Leroy Sievers, describes his experience:

> Every three weeks, I go up to the hospital at John Hopkins and I end up in a big room full of overstuffed chairs. There are TVs. The Price is Right seems to be a favorite. I am a regular now. Some people I recognize, and they recognize me, too. I feel bad when the hospital parking lot is full; that means a lot of sick people are in today.[38]

Remission and Recurrence

Patients receiving palliative treatment often are treated up until the end of their lives. Curative treatment, on the other hand, ceases when all evidence of cancer is gone. Patients may

Chemotherapy and Nerve Cells

Chemotherapy often damages nerve cells in the brain, arms, and legs. When nerve cells in the brain are damaged, people experience difficulty concentrating, memory loss, and lack of mental clarity. Damage to nerve cells in the arms and legs causes a condition known as peripheral neuropathy. Tingling and numbness in the fingers and toes characterize it. This can make it difficult for affected individuals to perform simple tasks like writing or dressing. Loss of feeling in the toes can also affect patients' sense of balance making them accident-prone. Loss of sensation also makes people less sensitive to heat, and therefore more likely to burn themselves. Some individuals are given medication to relieve these symptoms. Both mental confusion and peripheral neuropathy disappear when chemotherapy ends.

remain cancer-free for months or years. But there is always the possibility that lung cancer will recur, either in the lungs, or in other parts of the body where cancer cells that resisted the effects of treatment spread undetected. Doctors have no way of knowing whether this will happen. Therefore, patients with no evidence of cancer after treatment are said to be in remission. After five years without recurrence, the patient is considered cured.

If lung cancer recurs, chemotherapy is once again administered. Often a different combination of drugs is prescribed to combat resistant cancer cells. Some patients join clinical trials where new experimental drugs are used. However, the recurrence of lung cancer indicates that the cancer is aggressive and resistant to medication. This means once lung cancer recurs, it is likely to recur again. So the goal of treatment is to extend the period of remission. If the cancer recurs again, treatment is once again administered. Some people live with lung cancer for years controlling it in this manner, much like other people control chronic disease like diabetes or heart disease. "It's like diabetes," Donna says. "I'm not dying from my lung cancer, but it can't be cured. When it's acting up you treat it; when it isn't, you don't."[39]

Side Effects of Radiation and Chemotherapy

Any time lung cancer treatment is administered, whether initially or due to a recurrence, it can cause distressing side effects. Because chemotherapy and radiation introduce powerful substances into the body that stop cell division in both healthy and cancerous cells, they take a heavy toll on the body. Leroy Sievers puts it this way: "The idea is to poison the body enough to kill the cancer, but not quite kill the patient. Best I can tell, it's a difficult line to walk."[40]

Healthy cells that divide the fastest, such as red and white blood cells, those in hair follicles, and the digestive tract are most vulnerable. The most common side effects, including nausea and vomiting, loss of appetite, hair loss, fatigue, and a

Treatment

decrease in white and red blood cells, are associated with these cells. Although not all individuals react the same way to lung cancer treatment, and side effects end when treatment is over, digestive problems are widespread. Most people experience nausea and vomiting on the first two or three days of chemotherapy. Anti-nausea medication helps to control, but not completely eliminate, this problem. Feelings of nausea also lessen an individual's appetite, as do chemotherapy medications, which can deaden or change a person's sense of taste as well as cause individuals to have an unpleasant taste in their mouths. And radiation can burn the esophagus, making swallowing difficult. Aaron describes his experience: "The Tarceva [a chemotherapy medication] has clobbered my appetite. NOTHING tastes good. I feel like I could go without eating."[41]

Hair loss is another troubling side effect. Radiation and chemotherapy destroy cells in hair follicles, causing hair growing in the follicles to fall out. Radiation therapy causes hair loss

Both radiation treatment and chemotherapy have many side effects, the most visible being hair loss.

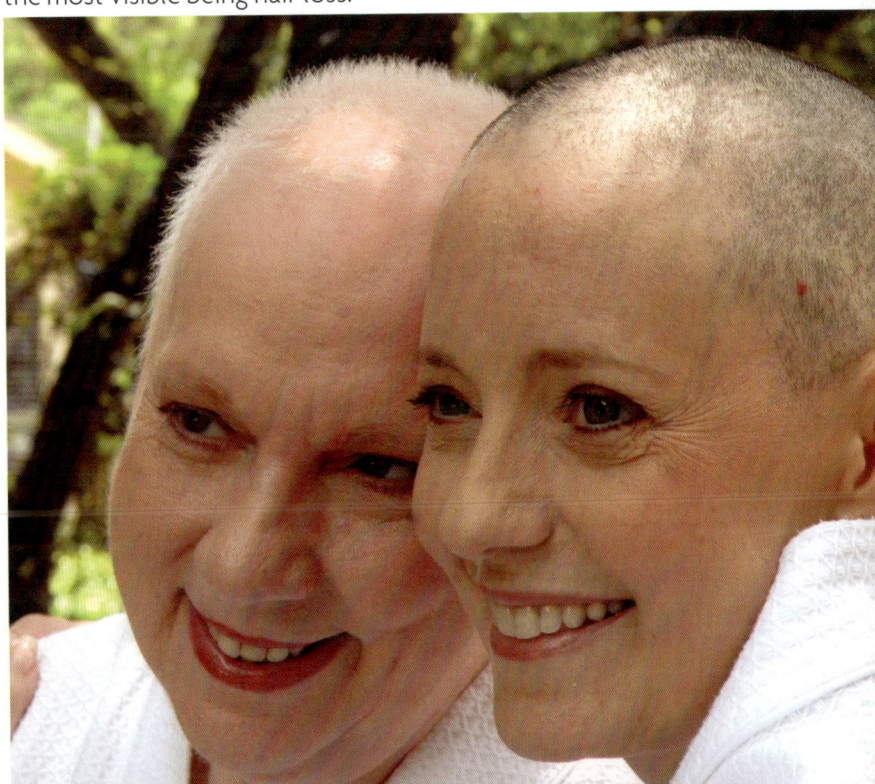

just in the area treated, while chemotherapy causes it all over the body. Diane, a lung cancer survivor, recalls what happened to her during chemotherapy: "By the second month, my hair started to fall out. I knew it was going to thin, but I had no idea how much I would lose. I ended up losing more than half."[42]

A decline in red and white blood cells is one more problem. Since the job of white blood cells is to fight infection, individuals are more vulnerable to contagious disease when white blood cell counts are depressed. When this happens, treatment is halted until the cell count normalizes. Aaron explains: "Chemotherapy, aside from killing cancer cells, kills white blood cells (wbc). Wbc's are those cute little cells that kill off infection, without them you could die. Mine were reduced to 1.0, regular counts are like 12.0."[43]

Lower red blood cell counts also lead to trouble. Red blood cells carry oxygen-rich hemoglobin, which the body needs for strength and energy. When red blood cell counts fall, individuals are easily fatigued. John, a lung cancer survivor, remembers:

> One side effect was fatigue. It hit me over the head from the first dose, and it was monumental. Other fatigue is treatable; when you're tired you take a nap or get a night's sleep. Those things do not work with radiation fatigue. You're just as tired when you get up from taking the rest. You're lying there; every pore of your body is lifeless.[44]

Complementary Alternative Treatment

To better cope with the side effects of lung cancer treatment and to strengthen their bodies, many individuals with lung cancer combine traditional cancer treatments with alternative treatments. This is known as complementary treatment.

Unlike traditional treatments, alternative treatments have not undergone rigorous testing to prove their safety and effectiveness. Nor does the Federal Drug Administration (FDA), a government agency that sets standards and regulates approved treatments, regulate them. Most healthcare professionals agree

Treatment

Besides undergoing the traditional medical treatments for cancer, many patients are also turning to alternative, complementary treatments, such as yoga, to help fight the disease.

that alternative treatments cannot replace conventional lung cancer treatment. But many do say that combining certain alternative treatments with standard lung cancer treatment can be beneficial. In fact, approximately 50 percent of the sixty-three National Cancer Institute cancer centers in the United States offer some form of alternative treatment. Former National Cancer Institute director Andrew C. von Eschenbach explains: "You're seeing an effort to complement the tried-and-true interventions with additional ones that may be helpful."[45]

There are a number of alternative complementary treatments that lung cancer patients turn to. These include nutritional supplements, herbal remedies, and acupuncture, to name a few.

But mind/body techniques such as guided imagery and meditation are among the most popular. They use the mind to calm the body and promote healing. While meditating, individuals recite a word or phrase in an effort to calm the mind. During guided imagery, a technique pioneered by oncologist O. Carl Simonton, individuals envision mental images of a particular goal. For example, many people imagine chemotherapy drugs going directly to a tumor and destroying it. Patients also use guided imagery to minimize the side effects of radiation and chemotherapy by visualizing themselves free of fatigue or digestive problems.

Although there is no conclusive proof that these practices work, a number of studies show them to be effective in reducing stress and anxiety caused by cancer treatments. And since stress causes the body to release cortisol, a hormone that interferes with the healing process, supporters of guided imagery and meditation say that by reducing stress these practices help enhance an individual's ability to heal. In fact, a 2000 study at Stanford University, Palo Alto, California found that cancer patients with the normal levels of cortisol lived a year longer than those with elevated levels of the hormone.

Indeed, some alternative treatments can help people cope with lung cancer treatment. Alternative treatments, however, cannot cure lung cancer. Only traditional treatments, no matter how distressing they may be, offer the chance of a cure. And whena cure is not possible, they can extend a person's life. Leroy Sievers puts it this way: "Every procedure, every dose of radiation, every drop of poison that goes into our arms, every thing we do has one goal... Keeping us alive. And every day that we wake up... is one more day that cancer can't have."[46]

CHAPTER FOUR

Living with Lung Cancer

Living with lung cancer is challenging. Individuals must cope with the toll lung cancer takes on their bodies, the side effects of treatment, and the emotional issues that having cancer can cause. By taking steps to meet these challenges, people with lung cancer gain control over their lives, which, in turn, improves the quality of their lives. Leroy Sievers puts it this way, "After that day, your life is never the same. 'That day' is the day the doctor tells you, 'You have cancer.' Every one of us knows someone who's had to face the news. It's scary; it's sad. But it's still life and it is a life worth living."[47]

Coping with Fatigue

Overwhelming fatigue caused by lung cancer, itself, as well as by lung cancer treatments, makes it difficult for people with lung cancer to maintain their normal lives. Although fatigue is a problem for individuals with all types of cancer, because of the involvement of the lungs, it is most pronounced in lung cancer. In fact, according to Henschke, McCarthy, and Wernick, most individuals with lung cancer say that fatigue is the most incapacitating problem linked to the disease. The authors explain: "Fatigue can interfere with your ability to think, steal your energy, and leave you unable to work or carry out everyday chores. It can rob you of your time with your loved ones and everything that makes life enjoyable."[48]

Lung Cancer Patients Should Quit Smoking

One of the most important steps lung cancer patients who are current smokers can take is to quit smoking. The National Cancer Institute found that smoking may reduce the effectiveness of cancer treatment and increase the chances of other forms of cancer developing. Moreover, smoking appears to worsen the side effects of cancer treatment, raise the risk of complications occurring after lung surgery, and shorten a lung cancer patient's lifespan. A 2001 study conducted by the National Cancer Institute compared survival rates of people with small cell lung cancer who continued to smoke after their diagnosis with those who did not. Those individuals who continued to smoke had a shorter survival time then those who quit smoking when they were diagnosed. The longest survival time went to those people who had stopped smoking at least 2.5 years before their diagnosis.

Maintaining a balance between activity and rest helps individuals with lung cancer to cope. This means taking frequent naps to preserve energy, as well as reducing regular activities. Such cutbacks often include reducing work hours or taking a leave of absence from work, curtailing social activities, and getting help with tasks like driving, housecleaning, shopping, cooking, and childcare from friends, family members, or professional caregivers. Donna explains:

I retired last February. Making that decision was hard. When I quit, I felt like I was giving in to the cancer. But I didn't have the energy to handle my career plus being a mother and a wife. Now I can nap in the afternoon and spend time later with my daughter… I miss my job terribly, but I know I did the right thing.[49]

While undergoing cancer treatment, it is important for a patient to maintain a balance between activity and rest.

Pain Management

Persistent pain can also cause overwhelming fatigue, along with sleeplessness, and depression. Soreness is common after surgery. Chemotherapy and radiation also causes pain in some people, as do tumors that press on nerves, bones, and organs. "I had almost no bone pain prior to chemo," Aaron says.

> My back was annoying, but I chalked it up to a bad night's sleep. Two days after my chemo stopped my back pain went from a 1 to a 9. It was throbbing and borderline debilitating. Now two weeks post chemo, the back pain has subsided mostly, but my chest (site of big tumor), and hip are up to 8/9.[50]

Taking prescribed pain medication helps people with lung cancer deal with pain. Participating in enjoyable activities that distract individuals from painful sensations also helps. Activities such as listening to music, watching a movie or favorite television show, visiting with family and friends, or pursuing a hobby all make it easier for lung cancer patients to take their mind off pain. Diane, a lung cancer survivor, recalls: "I became obsessed with old black and white movies, and would find myself disappearing into the past, mesmerized by the costumes, sets, and dialogue. Strangely, I got very attached to the contestants on *American Idol*!"[51]

Exercise, too, relieves pain. It also combats fatigue and strengthens weak muscles. Exercise stimulates the production of endorphins, natural chemicals that give exercisers a feeling of well-being, thereby reducing feelings of pain. Even though individuals with lung cancer might not feel well enough

As a way of combating the pain associated with lung cancer, some patients find it helpful to participate in low impact exercise like walking.

Living with Lung Cancer

to participate in vigorous exercise, doing low impact exercises such as walking, water exercises, tai chi, and yoga for five-minute intervals helps. According to the Lung Cancer Alliance,

> Fatigue, pain, and the emotional adjustment that may accompany major changes in your body ... take a toll. Many people have found that participating in some form of exercise helps them... Participation in low-impact activities ... can provide you with a renewed sense of wholeness and well-being.[52]

Coping with Breathing Difficulties

Exercise also helps people with lung cancer cope with breathing difficulties. The disease itself, damage caused by radiation, and surgical removal of lung tissue, all reduce a person's breathing capacity. This makes performing everyday tasks difficult and increases fatigue. Special breathing exercises help individuals take in more oxygen. Many people with lung cancer work with a respiratory therapist with whom they practice abdominal breathing. It is a special breathing exercise that uses the power of the diaphragm, the muscle under the lungs, to increase breathing capacity.

Mild physical exercise, such as a walking program, also helps. It builds up the lungs. Sharon, a lung cancer survivor who had a lobectomy, credits exercise with the improvement in her lung capacity:

> I started out exercising seriously about six weeks after my surgery and it was quite tough when I began. I swim, and I recall not having any reserve breath—I could not go very deep under the water because I absolutely had NO air within a matter of seconds. It was a very, very strange sensation. What I normally had before surgery just wasn't there. But the good news, that doesn't happen anymore. I'm not 100% and I don't dive real deep down and hang around bottoms of pools but I can do any normal thing

while swimming.... You will see huge, huge improvement as time goes on.[53]

Even with exercise, most people who have had part of their lungs removed do not regain maximum breathing capacity. They find that slowing down, pacing themselves, and taking frequent rests helps them to compensate. Don, a lung cancer survivor explains: "If I get active, I have to breathe harder than anyone else to keep going, I cut firewood, split firewood, tote it into the house, mow the lawn and work in the garden. All this stuff I can do, but I will have to take more rest breaks." [54]

If lung cancer has impaired a person's ability to breath easily, the use of a oxygen tank may be needed to help with the patient's breathing.

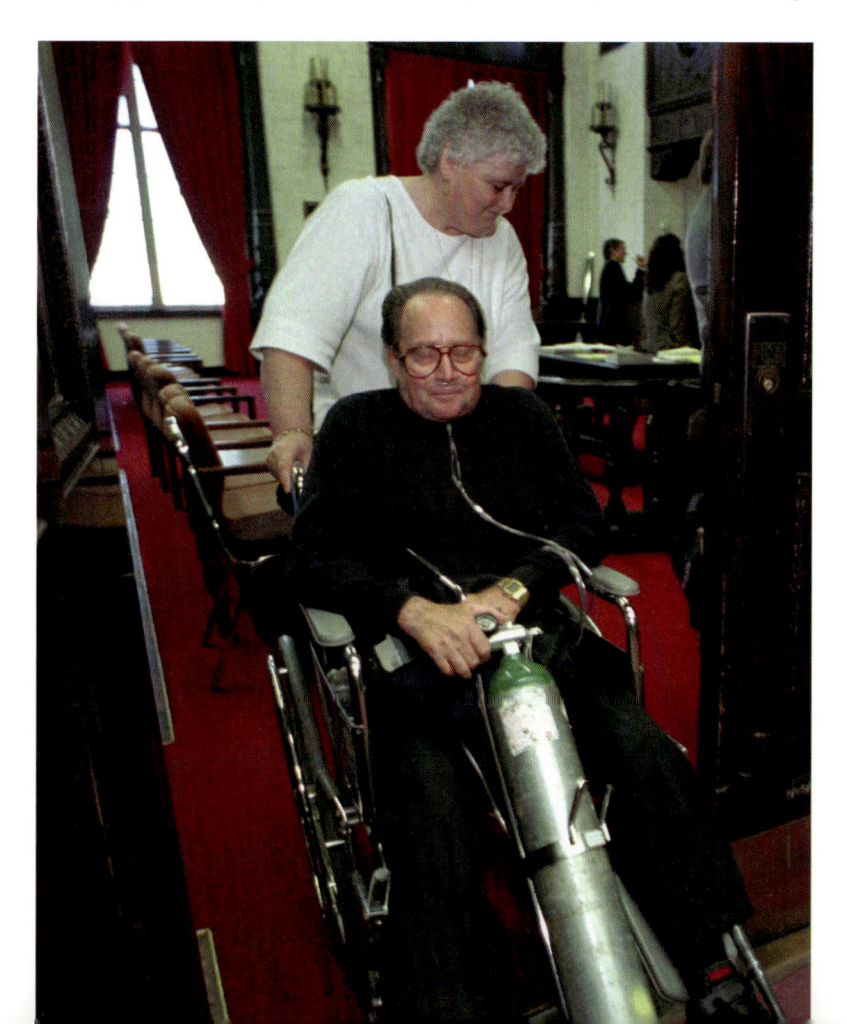

And if breathing capacity is severely impaired, undergoing oxygen therapy can help. This involves the use of an oxygen tank that delivers supplemental oxygen to people who cannot get enough oxygen on their own. The tank consists of a cylinder filled with compressed oxygen. The oxygen is usually delivered from the tank to thin plastic tubing that attaches under each of the patient's nostrils. The tank may be attached to a mobile IV pole, or it may be contained in a small portable tank light enough for users to carry with them when they leave home. Geri describes how her brother, who recently had lung cancer surgery, copes:

> Yesterday he (wheeling that oxygen tank with him) went to his daughter's softball game and home for dinner and then to his son's roller hockey game. We don't know if he will always need O2, but "there is life with a tank." I just wanted to say that the breathing problem is stressful and nerve wracking to say the least, but it can be dealt with.[55]

Avoiding Infection

Another challenge people with lung cancer face is the threat of infection. When chemotherapy and radiation deplete white blood cells, individuals are more susceptible to infection. Respiratory infections such as the flu or pneumonia that are usually not deadly in healthy people present a potentially lethal threat to the weakened lungs of lung cancer patients. Being vaccinated for the flu and pneumonia helps protect individuals from contracting these illnesses. "Don't wait to ask your doctor about getting vaccinated," authors Karen Parles and Joan H. Schiller, MD, advise lung cancer patients. "It could save your life."[56]

Other steps also help lung cancer patients to minimize the threat of infection when their white blood cell count drops. These include avoiding enclosed crowded areas in which germs can be spread easily, such as crowded movie theaters, malls, airports, elevators, restaurants, buses, trains, or airplanes, and avoiding contact with people who have recently had a contagious disease. Frequent hand washing, too, helps. It removes any germs lung cancer patients may have come in contact with. Washing dishes in a dishwasher on the hottest cycle is another way to guard against germs. Kathleen describes her experience while receiving chemotherapy: "The main concern for now is monitoring my white blood cell counts and hope they don't go too low. They suggest staying out of crowds and trying to avoid germs—for the next six months! I'll be hopelessly behind on the movies."[57]

Managing Appetite Problems

Nausea and vomiting caused by chemotherapy, and difficulty swallowing caused by radiation therapy present still more challenges. These issues, combined with the disease itself and the tendency of chemotherapy to affect the taste buds, leads many individuals with lung cancer to experience poor appetite. Lack of adequate nutrition weakens the immune system, causes fatigue, decreases strength and muscle mass, and leads to excess weight loss. Indeed, doctors estimate that individuals being treated for cancer need 20 percent more nutrients than healthy individuals because cancer, radiation, and chemotherapy deplete the body of nutrients. Moreover, getting adequate nutrition enhances the effectiveness of chemotherapy by making the body better able to absorb and tolerate the medication. Therefore, combating the problems that lead to poor appetite is essential to fighting lung cancer.

Taking anti-nausea drugs and medication that numbs the throat, making swallowing easier, are just two of the many measures people with lung cancer take to deal with these problems. Drinking plenty of fluids is another. Many chemotherapy patients find that drinking at least a gallon of water or juice each day for two days before going into chemotherapy reduces nausea. Fluids help flush excess chemotherapy drugs out of the digestive tract. Otherwise, they linger causing nausea and vomiting. Being well hydrated also prevents constipation, a side effect of anti-nausea medication, as well as reducing fatigue, a symptom of dehydration.

Eating soft cold foods such as yogurt, puddings, cottage cheese, and ice cream eases swallowing problems by numbing the throat. Substituting liquid nourishment for solid food also makes swallowing easier, and is better tolerated by a queasy stomach. Commercial liquid food supplements and homemade fruit smoothies and shakes, prepared with fresh produce, milk, and protein powder, provide much-needed calories that prevent weight loss and valuable nutrients that improve healing. For instance, vitamins and minerals in fruit enhance the immune system, while the body uses protein to repair itself. Getting adequate protein is especially important for people with cancer, who need the nutrients to repair damage to healthy cells destroyed by cancer treatment.

Drinking plenty of water while undergoing treatment for lung cancer, may help a patient cope with several of the unpleasant side effects of the treatment, such as nausea and vomiting.

Eating five or six small, light meals throughout the day also helps. Many individuals who do not have the appetite for three heavy meals find this eating pattern more tolerable. Adding nutritious high-calorie toppings like cheese and nuts to these light meals helps patients fight weight loss, as does carrying nutritious snacks wherever they go. That way, food is readily available whenever they do feel hungry. And some individuals find that going to a restaurant or dining with friends makes eating more pleasurable.

Taking a walk or doing other light physical activity about one hour before eating also stimulates the appetite. Aaron found that a session at the YMCA helped boost his appetite. After one visit, he reported: "I did 46 minutes on the bike... Worked up an appetite. Made an open face tuna sandwich with goat cheese, scallions, and tomatoes on toasted wheat bread. Washed down with a fruit smoothie (two kiwis, one banana, a peach, apple juice, soy protein). Eating like this I feel like I can do anything."[58]

Coping with Hair Loss

Hair loss presents another type of challenge. Because it affects a person's appearance it can be disheartening. Hair loss, especially on women, visibly marks an individual as a cancer patient. It becomes a daily reminder to patients and to others of how the disease has taken control over the patient's life. As a result, many individuals report that hair loss lowers their self-confidence and impacts the way others interact with them.

A 2006 survey of women throughout the Unites States with cancer conducted by the Look Good... Feel Better program, an organization that helps individuals with cancer cope with changes in their appearance, found nearly half the women surveyed said that since their hair loss others treated them differently. And 83 percent said that hair loss had a negative impact on the quality of their lives. Kristen, a cancer survivor, puts it this way:

Living with Lung Cancer

I wanted to be as normal as possible. I needed to keep me. I did not want to invite people into my world by my appearance. Cancer treatments are so in your face—literally! Every morning and every night I face the harsh reality of those treatments… The way I look says a lot about me and about the way I feel.[59]

The survey also found that 86 percent of those surveyed said that taking steps to improve their appearance made them feel better. Preparing for hair loss ahead of time is one such step. Many lung cancer patients find that getting a short haircut before they begin chemotherapy makes this transition easier, while some shave their heads entirely. Lung cancer survivor Deborah recalls:

A cancer patient being fitted with a wig. Once hair loss occurs due to cancer treatment, a wig is a way to make a patient feel more confident until her hair grows back.

In July, I had my second round of chemotherapy. I began to lose my hair. This was an emotional part of my treatment; however, I decided to take hold of the situation. I was not going to let lung cancer take control of me. I called my hair stylist to set up an appointment to cut my hair as short as possible. He gave me a GI haircut… I could now focus on the big picture: "fighting the cancer."[60]

Once hair loss occurs many individuals wear wigs, toupees, caps, hats, or scarves, until their hair grows back. Cindy recalls: "When I choose wigs, I would pick looks not at all like my own hairstyle to make it fun rather than scary."[61]

Organizations such as the American Cancer Organization pay for wigs, and groups like Look Good… Feel Better offer female patients group and individual sessions throughout the United States with hair care and beauty professionals. At these sessions cancer patients are taught how to style wigs, wrap turbans, and scarves, and how to apply make-up to problem areas like lost eyelashes and eyebrows. "Our goal," says Louanne Roark vice president of Look Good… Feel Better, "is to make Look Good… Feel Better a part of every cancer patient's treatment.experience, giving them the tools they need to take control of the appearance-related effects of cancer treatment and creating a sense of hope and self-determination."[62]

Emotional Distress

Hair loss is not the only emotional issue lung cancer patients face. Lung cancer treatments are stressful, and even when treatments are over, individuals with lung cancer cope with many emotional challenges. Despite the fact that an individual may be in remission, the threat of recurrence is always there. In order to determine whether a patient is cancer free and healthy, frequent medical monitoring including doctor visits, blood tests, and CAT scans are required. Generally, individuals are checked every three months for the first two years, then every six months for the next three years, and annually thereafter. If the cancer has recurred, it is likely to be discovered during these visits. That is what happened to Anita. She recalls: "I had regular scans over the next few years and everything looked fine. Then, six years after my diagnosis, I was diagnosed with another spot on my lungs."[63]

Therefore, each doctor visit brings with it uncertainty and emotional stress. "All scan days are difficult," Leroy Sievers says. "Waiting for the results is excruciating. A good scan day is like your birthday and Christmas rolled into one. A bad scan day sends your life careening off in another direction. And each time that happens, things seem to get worse."[64]

Even when tests yield favorable results, knowing that the disease can recur at any time and the recurrence could be fatal takes a tremendous emotional toll on lung cancer survivors. Lea puts it this way: "My prognosis for the moment is good. However, I get CT scans every year and I keep my fingers crossed until I get the results. I guess you never really feel as though you're out of the woods."[65]

As a consequence, many lung cancer patients suffer from depression. Stress and depression not only lower a person's quality of life, they also cause insomnia and poor appetite, and they lessen the immune system's ability to fight infection. To help cope with emotional issues many individuals with lung cancer seek the help of a mental health professional, who provides them with an outlet to express their concerns. Antidepressant medications also help individuals to feel better and gain control over their emotions.

Support Groups

Joining a support group is another way people with lung cancer cope with emotional issues. Participating in a support group gives individuals an opportunity to discuss their feelings and anxieties and share their experiences with other cancer patients. Groups may consist only of lung cancer patients, or be a mix of people with all kinds of cancer. In a group setting, individuals express their feelings and exchange information and advice about fighting and living with lung cancer. Karen, a cancer survivor, puts it this way:

What is a Hospice?

When all treatment has failed and lung cancer patients are facing the end of their lives, many turn to hospice care. In the past, the word hospice referred to a refuge or guesthouse for sick or weary travelers. Today, a hospice provides care for terminally ill patients who are expected to live six months or less. Care may be provided in the patient's home or in a special hospice center. Hospice care is not concerned with curative care or prolonging life. Instead, it tries to make terminally ill patients comfortable. Pain management, therefore, is an important part of hospice care.

A team of professionals visits and works with hospice patients. Doctors, nurses, religious advisors, social workers, counselors, psychologists, and trained volunteers all may be part of this team. Their goal is to give patients and their families medical, emotional, and spiritual comfort and support so they can deal with end-of-life issues more easily. The hospice team also helps family members deal with their loss after the patient's death.

A terminal cancer patient in hospice gets her picture taken with family members during a dinner celebration.

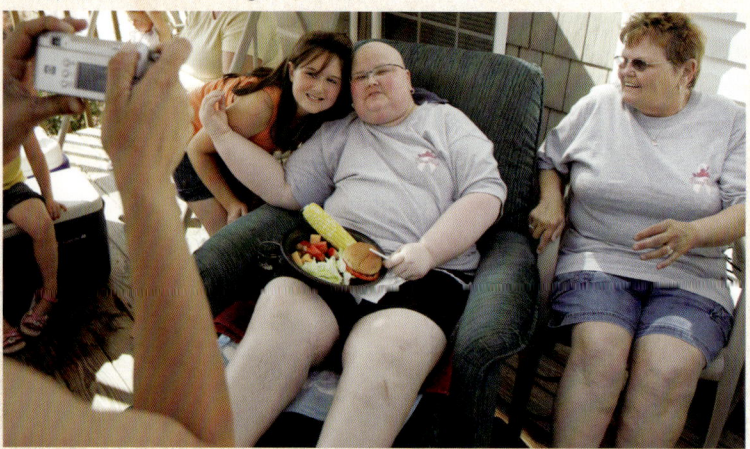

A support group can help you overcome your own sense of vulnerability. Of course, your mortality is thrown in your face, but the hardest part for me... you are basically out of control of your life.... No one understands that as well as someone who has experienced it.[66]

Support groups can be found everywhere. Many hospitals sponsor support groups, as do community organizations and religious institutions. There are even internet support groups for people who are unable to leave their homes.

Indeed, participating in a support group is just one of the many steps people with lung cancer take to improve the quality of their lives. Although living with lung cancer is challenging, individuals who take steps to meet these challenges feel happier and more in control of their lives. Five-year stage IV lung cancer survivor Sharon puts it this way: "I'm not dying of cancer, I'm living with it... It's a great life if you don't weaken."[67]

CHAPTER FIVE

What the Future Holds

Scientists and healthcare professionals are taking a multifaceted approach to dealing with lung cancer. First, they are taking steps to educate the public to the dangers of smoking, and passing laws to limit exposure to second hand smoke. In this way, they expect to reduce new cases of lung cancer in the future. Secondly, by advocating for early screening, and developing easier and more effective screening devices, they hope to detect more lung cancer cases in their earliest stages, when the disease is most curable. Finally, they are working on developing a lung cancer vaccine and a new form of treatment that would target lung cancer cells without damaging healthy cells.

Smoking Prevention

Since smoking is the main cause of lung cancer, healthcare professionals, government officials, educators, and concerned citizens are all working together to keep people from starting to smoke and encourage smokers to quit. "The key to preventing lung cancer is smoking prevention and cessation," say Parles and Schiller.[68]

School-based prevention programs are a key part of this effort. From kindergarten through high school, students receive anti-smoking education as part of their health education curriculum. Guest speakers, role playing, and multicultural videos produced by groups like the American Cancer Association are all part of the curriculum. Celebrities also contribute. Many classrooms are decorated with posters that feature sports stars

What the Future Holds

like skateboarder Tony Hawk, Brazilian soccer star Sisi, and World Cup champion mountain biker Alison Dunlap, to name a few, urging young people not to smoke.

Anti-smoking campaigns in the media are also a part of the prevention program. Public service announcements, newspaper and magazine articles, and billboards all warn people about the danger of smoking. So far, this multi-pronged approach seems to be working. Explains Ronald Natale, MD: "The education campaign we've had over the last 30 years has reduced cigarette smoking from 50 percent among men down to about 25 percent of the United States."[69]

Smoking Cessation Programs

Despite the decrease in the number of smokers in the United States, according to the American Lung Association, every day an estimated forty-eight hundred Americans age eleven to seventeen smoke their first cigarette. Many go on to become regular smokers. To help young Americans break the habit, the American Lung Association developed Not on Tobacco (N-O-T). This smoking cessation program is offered to schools, youth groups, and community organizations throughout the

Scarlott Mueller, chairperson and president of the American Cancer Society, Florida Division, speaks at a news conference introducing a youth tobacco education program.

United States and provides guidance and support, as well as practical lessons in decision-making and stress management skills to young smokers.

Other programs are geared to people of all ages. Hospitals, local governments, and community organizations offer smoking cessation programs. Support groups provide encouragement and assistance. There are even internet support groups such as QuitNet.com that bring together people throughout the world who are trying to quit smoking. The American Cancer Society also offers on-line assistance, which includes advice on how to quit, tips on how to deal with tobacco cravings, and contact information for counselors who are available day or night to help people trying to quit. According to the National Cancer Institute:

The Great American Smoke-Out

The Great American Smoke Out occurs every year on the third Thursday in November. Sponsored by the American Cancer Society, the event aims to help people stop smoking. On the Great American Smoke-Out Day, people give up cigarettes for twenty-four hours.

The event began in Minnesota in the early 1970s. It quickly spread to other states. In 1977, the American Cancer Society made it a national event. Educational programs, parades, guest appearances by celebrities who quit smoking, ceremonial cigarette burials, and pep rallies are all part of the festivities.

As many as one-third of American smokers participate in the smoke-out. When they see they can go without cigarettes for the day, many are encouraged to quit permanently. Healthcare experts agree that when it comes to preventing lung cancer and reducing lung cancer deaths, smoking cessation is second only to not starting.

What the Future Holds

People who quit smoking live longer than those who continue to smoke... About 10 years after quitting, an ex-smoker's risk of dying from lung cancer is 30 percent to 50 percent less than the risk for those who continue to smoke... Quitting smoking reduces the risk for developing cancer, and this benefit increases the longer a person remains smoke free.[70]

Making Smoking More Difficult

Lawmakers supported by concerned citizens and healthcare professionals are also taking a stand. They are passing laws that make acquiring cigarettes and smoking in public places more difficult. This, they say, will discourage people from smoking

Former basketball star Alonzo Mourning signs a pledge to never begin smoking during a rally to kick-off the Great American Smokeout.

and limit non-smokers' exposure to second-hand smoke. For example, many state governments have been raising excise taxes on the sale of cigarettes in hopes that the higher price of cigarettes will keep young people from beginning to smoke and encourage smokers to quit. In addition, all fifty states prohibit the sale of tobacco to minors. Sellers are fined. And in forty-five states minors caught purchasing tobacco face stiff penalties that include a suspended driver's license, community service, and/or mandatory attendance in a smoking cessation program.

By passing laws against vending machines, cities, too, are making it more difficult for everyone, and especially minors, to get cigarettes. In fifty-four cities, cigarette vending machines are against the law. Other cities have regulations that require that vending machines have a lock-out device. In order to purchase cigarettes from such machines, buyers have to show a store clerk identification that proves they are over 18. Only then will the clerk remove the lock out device.

Other laws restrict smoking in public places. Countries throughout the world, including Great Britain, France, Italy,

Worldwide Statistics on Tobacco Use

Estimated number of people who die each year from smoking.	5 million
Estimated number of people who will die each year from smoking, by the year 2030.	10 million
Number of cigarettes smoked worldwide per day.	15 billion
Percentage of men in developing countries who smoke.	50 percent
Percentage of women in developing countries who smoke.	9 percent
Estimated cost to the global economy of smoking, per year.	$200 billion dollars

Source: American Lung Association. Available online at: http://www.lungusa.org/site/pp.asp?c=dvLUK9O0E&b=39860.

What the Future Holds

Ireland, Denmark, Australia, Bhutan, and the United States, have some type of smoke-free air laws. For instance, all fifty of the United States and the District of Columbia ban smoking in government buildings. As of July 2007, thirty-eight states ban smoking in public and private workplaces. Fourteen states have laws that prohibit smoking in all public places.

Such bans make smoking less socially acceptable, which, experts say, makes it less appealing to start smoking and motivates current smokers to quit. Indeed, one month after the state of Washington prohibited smoking in public places, the state's quit-smoking phone hotline reported an 80 percent increase in calls. According to Stanton Glantz, director of the Center for Tobacco Control Research and Education at the University of California, San Francisco,

> When you make workplaces, public places, restaurants and bars smoke free, people smoke less. They sell fewer cigarettes. Workplace bans, especially, can have a dramatic effect. We've consistently found that you get a 30 percent drop in cigarette consumption when you make a workplace smoke-free. About half of that is people cutting down and about half of it is [people] quitting.[71]

At the same time, smoke-free air laws reduce non-smokers' exposure to carcinogens. A 2004 study conducted by the Roswell Park Cancer Institute in Buffalo, New York compared the level of carcinogens in the air in restaurants and bars in New Jersey, where smoking was permitted at that time, to that in New York City, where it was banned. The results of the study showed that workers and customers in the smoking venues were exposed to more than nine times the level of carcinogens as those in the non-smoking venues. According to Jonathan Foulds, the Director of the Tobacco Dependence Program at the University of Medicine and Dentistry of New Jersey (UMDNJ)-School of Public Health, "These results indicate that ... the environment in these bars and restaurants is really unhealthy. In fact,

A sign in a St. Paul, Minnesota, restaurant informs diners that smoking is no longer permitted in the establishment. As of July 2007, fourteen states have laws that prohibit smoking in all public places.

for people who work in these polluted environments on a daily basis, it could mean the difference between whether or not they contract a serious disease."[72]

Lung cancer expert Mark Kris M,D, agrees:

> Any efforts that make it harder to smoke decrease the number of cigarettes smoked by individuals and the number of individuals that smoke at all. Everyone interested in fighting lung cancer should support bans of smoking everywhere. If smoking is curtailed, lung cancer will be curtailed as well.[73]

Early Diagnosis

Healthcare professionals and lung cancer advocates are taking another approach to curtail the impact of lung cancer. Currently early-screening tests for breast, colon, cervical, and prostate cancers are part of routine physical exams. In fact, they are usually paid for by health insurance plans. Such testing makes early detection more likely, which healthcare professionals say is one reason why survival and cure rate of these diseases have increased significantly. In addition, finding these cancers early has helped scientists understand these diseases better, which saves lives. For example, early screening for colon cancer has made scientists aware that polyps or benign growths in the colon almost always develop before cancer tumors. Removing these growths can prevent the disease from developing.

It is not surprising, then, that many lung cancer experts believe that routine screening for lung cancer would yield similar results. Harvey Pass, MD and professor of surgery and oncology at Wayne State University in Detroit explains: "The future of lung cancer management lies in early detection."[74]

Currently some physicians administer a chest x-ray as part of a routine physical, but many do not. While a chest x-ray is a valuable tool, it misses an estimated 85 percent of stage I lung cancer. On the other hand, modern CT scans can produce up to

600 high-resolution images of the lungs in a single scan, making detecting tiny stage I tumors possible. A thirteen-year study, which began in 1993, examined just how effective such scanning can be. The study, known as the International Early Lung Cancer Action Program, was conducted at 38 healthcare facilities throughout the world. As part of the study, 31,567 symptom-free people at high risk of developing lung cancer were administered a CT scan. The researchers detected many cases of early stage lung cancer, which would otherwise have probably gone undetected until symptoms developed and the disease had advanced. Of those individuals diagnosed with lung cancer, 80 percent had a ten-year survival rate, as opposed to the current five-year survival rate of 15 percent. Moreover, those patients in which the tumors were surgically removed had a 92 percent survival rate.

A CT scan of a cancer tumor in the left lower lung. Studies have found that CT scans are effective tools in diagnosing lung cancer early and increasing a patient's chance for survival.

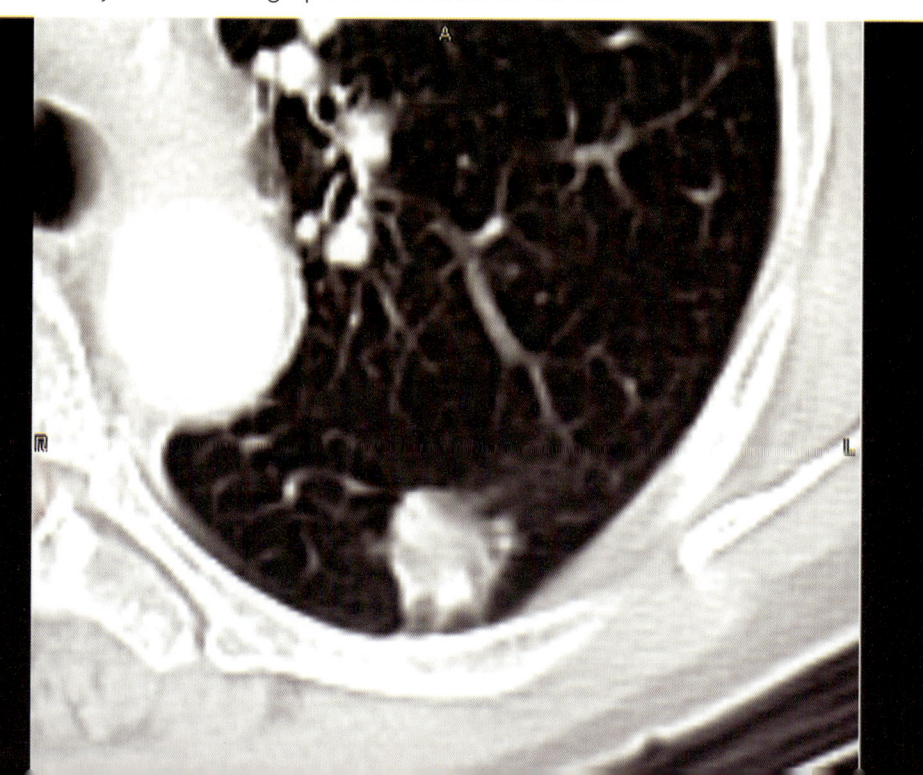

What the Future Holds

Despite these results, some scientists question the study's validity. Because the researchers did not include a control group of similar subjects who were not scanned and compare the mortality rates of the two groups, some scientists say the results are questionable. Other healthcare professionals have additional concerns. They say that because scans have such high resolution, routine scans are likely to detect tiny benign growths common on the lungs of smokers. Such growths look so much like early stage tumors that they are likely to be diagnosed as such, leading to unnecessary biopsies and anxiety for patients.

Advocates for routine scans disagree. They feel the benefits far outweigh the risks. Claudia I. Henschke who developed a low dose radiation CT scan and used it to scan 1,000 patients in a study similar to the International Early Lung Cancer Action Program, explains:

> We believe that when the promise of early detection becomes a widespread reality, annual lung cancer deaths could be cut in half. When this happens the total number of cancer deaths will drop significantly. Indeed, early detection of lung cancer promises to have a greater impact on the war against cancer than any other single factor on the horizon.[75]

A Lung Cancer Breath Test

While CT scans provide one way to detect lung cancer in its early stages, until the controversy that surrounds their use for this purpose is settled, they are not likely to be widely instituted as part of annual physical exams. Therefore, scientists are working on developing other lung cancer screening tools, such as a lung cancer breath test. Such a test would not require expensive equipment or expose patients to radiation, and it is less likely to produce false positive results. With this in mind, scientists at the Cleveland Clinic in Ohio have built a breathalyzer, which they say could make early detection of lung cancer the norm.

The scientists already knew that cancer cells produce chemicals known as volatile organic compounds, which normal cells do not produce. Machines known as mass spectrometers can detect these chemicals. But mass spectrometers are very large, complicated, and expensive, making them impractical for everyday use. Therefore, the scientists set out to develop a simpler method of detection. What they came up with is a disposable piece of paper, about the size of a quarter, with 36 chemically-treated spots. The spots are designed to change color according to the compounds they come in contact with. Volatile organic compounds, the scientists theorized, would cause the spots to produce a specific color pattern.

In 2006, the scientists tested the effectiveness of the device on 143 people, some of whom were healthy and some of whom were known to have lung cancer. Each subject breathed into a device that contained the treated paper for twelve minutes. A computer then scanned the papers, looking for a specific color pattern. The test identified the people with lung cancer

A researcher testing DNA in a laboratory in Salt Lake City, Utah. Researchers are hoping that by analyzing DNA they can diagnose a person with lung cancer before the tumor actually develops.

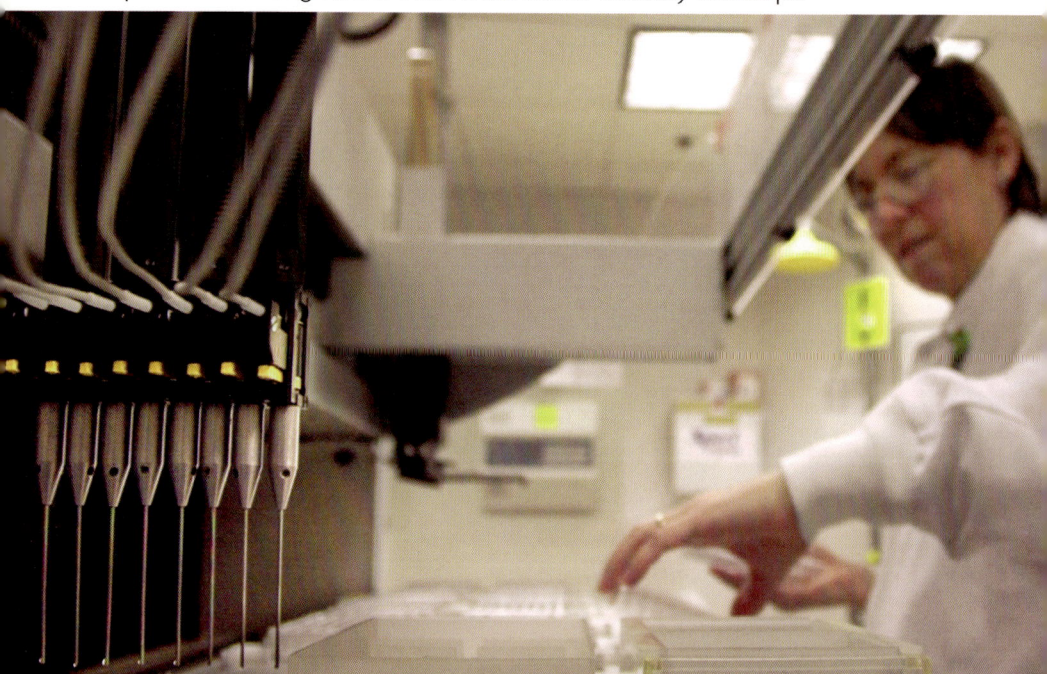

72 percent of the time. It also correctly identified 73 percent of the healthy subjects.

The scientists are currently working on trying to make the test even more effective. They hope to accomplish this by identifying the exact compounds contained in the breath of lung cancer patients. If they can do this, they can then treat the test paper with chemicals specific to these compounds. "Ultimately, this line of investigation could lead to an inexpensive, noninvasive screening or diagnostic test for lung cancer," the researchers say.[76]

Analyzing DNA

Volatile organic compounds are not the only substances in the breath of lung cancer patients that scientists are interested in. Scientists at the New York State Department of Health's Wadsworth Center in Albany theorize that by analyzing DNA, the genetic material found in every cell, in the breath of people with lung cancer they should be able to detect cancerous and even precancerous genetic changes in lung cells.

The researchers have already determined that tiny amounts of DNA can be extracted from cooled exhaled breath. They also know that when mucus coughed up by people with lung cancer is analyzed for genetic abnormalities, the mucus frequently contains mutated tumor suppression genes. These are the genes that signal cells to stop growing and are therefore central to the cancer process. However, since many people with lung cancer do not cough up mucus until the disease has advanced, analyzing coughed-up mucus is not a promising tool for early detection of the disease. But, the scientists hypothesized, if the breath of people with lung cancer also contain mutated or missing tumor suppressor genes, such analysis could be used to detect the illness early, as well as identifying people at risk of developing lung cancer in the future.

To test their theory, in 2007, the researchers analyzed the cooled exhaled breath of 33 people with and without lung cancer. The scientists found that the breath of the subjects with lung cancer had more mutated or non-functioning tumor suppressor genes than the breath of healthy individuals.

Next the scientists hope to compare the genetic pattern found in the breath of lung cancer patients to that in cancerous lung tissue. If they match, the scientists will be assured that such a genetic pattern in a person's breath does indeed indicate the presence of lung cancer, or the likelihood of the disease developing. As a result, DNA breath analysis could become a valuable early detection tool in the future. "This approach is innovative and creative," says Louis Weiner, MD, the moderator of a news conference at the 2007 annual meeting of the American Association for Cancer Research. "Down the road, this could prove to be a real winner."[77]

A Lung Cancer Vaccine

While some scientists are investigating ways to detect lung cancer, others are working on ways of preventing it from ever developing. Scientists at the University of Louisville in Kentucky are developing a lung cancer vaccine using embryonic stem cells. Stem cells are non-specific cells that are capable of changing into and repairing any cell in the body. Embryonic stem cells produce a number of proteins, some of which lung cancer tumors also produce. The scientists theorized that if they could develop a vaccine that triggered an immune response to stem cells, because of these shared proteins, such a vaccine would also prompt the immune system to attack lung cancer cells. This would keep the disease from ever developing.

In 2006, the scientists tested the vaccine on mice. The scientists injected the vaccine into one group of mice and used another group as a control. Then, they transplanted lung cancer cells under the animal's skin. One hundred percent of the control group developed lung cancer as compared to 20 percent of the vaccinated group.

Scientists are encouraged by the results, but since other vaccines have proven effective in protecting mice from cancer but have not worked on humans, they think a human vaccine

An Interesting Diagnostic Tool

Scientists at the Pine Street Foundation, San Anselmo, California are investigating whether dogs can smell volatile organic compounds found in the breath of lung and breast cancer patients. Because of previous studies, the scientists know that dogs can detect melanoma, a form of skin cancer, by smelling volatile organic compounds on skin lesions. However, detecting the compounds in a person's breath would be more difficult since they are significantly diluted. The scientists hoped that the dogs' keen sense of smell would overcome this challenge.

In 2006, the scientists gathered breath samples from 86 cancer patients, 55 with lung cancer and 31 with breast cancer, as well as samples from 83 healthy people. The dogs, trained to sit if they detected cancer, were given the samples to sniff. Depending on the dog, the animals correctly detected cancer between 88 and 97 percent of the time.

Some scientists say that dogs could be used in doctor's offices in the future; while others hope to develop technology that could detect cancer by scent.

In a 2006 study, dogs were used to diagnose lung and breast cancer by sniffing a patient's breath. The dogs correctly detected cancer between 88 and 97 percent of the time.

is still a long way off. Moreover, although the vaccine caused no problems in the mice, scientist do not know whether injecting live stem cells into humans would cause the body to attack its own stem cells, which could be dangerous. The researchers, therefore, are proceeding with caution. Study director John Eaton explains: "At present, all I can say is that so far it looks good, and that, unless something unexpected happens, this strategy might someday be applied to humans at high risk of developing cancer."[78]

Targeted Treatment

Another vaccine with a different goal is currently being tested in clinical trials on thirteen hundred people with lung cancer in thirty countries. This vaccine does not prevent lung cancer. Instead, it treats lung cancer by targeting lung cancer cells while leaving healthy cells unaffected. For this reason, it causes fewer side effects than chemotherapy or radiation. The vaccine targets a protein called MUC-1 that is produced by lung cancer cells. Once injected, the vaccine floods the body with segments of the protein, which the immune system recognizes as a hostile foreign invader. Consequently, the immune system launches an attack on lung cancer cells.

An earlier clinical trial tested the vaccine on 131 patients with recurring lung cancer. Half the patients were treated with chemotherapy plus the vaccine, while the other half received chemotherapy plus a placebo or fake vaccine. Then their survival rates were compared. The group that received the vaccine and chemotherapy survived thirty months or longer. The control group survived thirteen months or longer. The current trials are following the same procedure. Scientists do not think that this particular vaccine is strong enough to be used as a sole cancer treatment. But they do think that it may be an effective maintenance therapy that would prolong the lives of people with inoperable lung cancer following standard treatment. And, they hope to develop other targeted vaccines that can be used on their own in the future.

What the Future Holds

Lung cancer is a serious disease that kills a large number of people each year. Individuals in all walks of life are working hard to change that. Smoking prevention and cessation programs, early detection tools, a vaccine that prevents lung cancer, and targeted treatments that prolong life make it possible that someday lung cancer will not be as prevalent or as lethal. "I believe," says lung cancer expert Michael Vincent Smith, MD, "it is a future filled with hope."[79]

Notes

Introduction: The Forgotten Cancer
1. Quoted in Claudia I. Henschke, Peggy McCarthy, and Sarah Wernick, *Lung Cancer Myths, Facts, Choices—and Hope*. New York: W.W. Norton & Co, 2002, p. 15.
2. Quoted in Lorraine Johnston, *Lung Cancer Making Sense of Diagnosis, Treatment & Options*. Sebastopol, CA: O'Reilly, 2001, p. 250.
3. Quoted in The Healing Project, ed., *Voices of Lung Cancer*. Brooklyn, NY: LaChance Publishing, 2007, p. 31.
4. Quoted in Johnston, *Lung Cancer Making Sense of Diagnosis, Treatment & Options*, p. 251.
5. Quoted in Lung Cancer Alliance, "Faces in the Fight." www.lungcanceralliance.org/press/faceinthefight/index.html.
6. Sandy Phillips Britt, "Plea from a Dying Woman: Get a Second Opinion," *San Francisco Chronicle*, February 4, 2007, p. E3.

Chapter 1: What is Lung Cancer?
7. MIT World, "How Cancer Begins." http://mitworld.mit.edu/video/151/.
8. Robert A. Weinberg, *One Renegade Cell: How Cancer Begins*. New York: Basic Books, 1999, p. 3.
9. Weinberg, *One Renegade Cell*, p. 1.
10. Wheresmyp53, "Killing One Cancer Cell at a Time," October 23, 2006. http://wheresmyp53.blogspot.com/2006_10_01_archive.html.
11. Quoted in The Healing Project, ed., *Voices of Lung Cancer*, p. 35.
12. Quoted in CNN.com, "CNN Larry King Live," April 25, 2005. http://transcripts.cnn.com/TRANSCRIPTS/0504/05/lkl.01.html.

Notes

13. People Living with Cancer, "Q&A: Living With Lung Cancer," November 27, 2006. www.plwc.org/portal/site/PLWC/menuitem.169f5d85214941ccfd748f68ee37a01d/?vgnextoid=160c5057119ce010VgnVCM100000ed730ad1RCRD.
14. Quoted in The Healing Project, ed., *Voices of Lung Cancer*, p. 43.
15. People Living with Cancer, "Q&A: Living With Lung Cancer," November 15, 2006.
16. Quoted in Henschke, McCarthy, and Wernick, *Lung Cancer Myths, Facts, Choices—and Hope*, p. 65.
17. Quoted in United States Department of Health and Human Services, "Surgeon General Issues National Health Release on Radon," January 13, 2005. www.surgeongeneral.gov/pressreleases/sg01132005.html.
18. Quoted in Henschke, McCarthy, and Wernick, *Lung Cancer Myths, Facts, Choices—and Hope*, p. 60.
19. Lauren Terrazano, *Newsday*, "Cancer Rising Among Smoke and Mirrors," April 17, 2007.
20. Phillips Britt, "Plea from a Dying Woman: Get a Second Opinion."

Chapter 2: Symptoms and Diagnosis

21. Henschke, McCarthy, and Wernick, *Lung Cancer Myths, Facts, Choices—and Hope*, p. 2.
22. Phillips Britt, "Plea from a Dying Woman: Get a Second Opinion."
23. Cindy Bass, Lung Cancer.org, "Faces of Lung Cancer." www.lungcancer.org/patients/faces_of_lc/faces_of_lc_c_bass.htm.
24. Anita Johnson, Lung Cancer.org, "Faces of Lung Cancer." www.lungcancer.org/patients/faces_of_lc/faces_of_lc_a_johnston.htm.
25. Quoted in CNN.com, "CNN Larry King Live," April 25, 2005.
26. Quoted in Johnston, *Lung Cancer Making Sense of Diagnosis, Treatment & Options*, pp. 8-9.
27. Henschke, McCarthy, and Wernick, *Lung Cancer Myths, Facts, Choices—and Hope*, p.105.

28. Quoted in Johnston, *Lung Cancer Making Sense of Diagnosis, Treatment & Options*, p. 6.
29. Henschke, McCarthy, and Wernick, *Lung Cancer Myths, Facts, Choices—and Hope*, pp. 1–2.
30. Lung Cancer Survivor, "Francine Pesca Noce," November 15, 2006. http://lungcancer survivor.eblog.com/category/uncategorized/.
31. Quoted in The Healing Project, ed, *Voices of Lung Cancer*, p. 82.
32. Quoted in Johnston, *Lung Cancer Making Sense of Diagnosis, Treatment & Options*, pp. 88–89.

Chapter 3: Treatment

33. Quoted in Johnston, *Lung Cancer Making Sense of Diagnosis, Treatment & Options*, p.145
34. Quoted in The Healing Project, ed., *Voices of Lung Cancer*, p. 102.
35. Quoted in Erin Allday, *San Francisco Chronicle*, "As Lung Cancer Kills More Women a Call for Better Diagnosis, Care," November 17, 2006, p. A1. www.sfgate.com/cgi-bin/article.cgi?file=/c/a/2006/11/17/MNG5AMEO0T1.DTL.
36. Quoted in Henschke, McCarthy, and Wernick, *Lung Cancer Myths, Facts, Choices—and Hope*, p. 193.
37. Quoted in Johnston, *Lung Cancer Making Sense of Diagnosis, Treatment & Options*, p.131.
38. Leroy Sievers, NPR.org, "My Cancer," May 11, 2006. www.npr.org/blogs/mycancer/2006/05/.
39. Quoted in Henschke, McCarthy, and Wernick, *Lung Cancer Myths, Facts, Choices—and Hope*, p. 274.
40. Sievers, "My Cancer," May 11, 2006.
41. Wheresmyp53, "Killing Cancer One Cell at a Time," February 11, 2007. http://wheresmyp53.blogspot.com/2007_02_01_archive.html.
42. Quoted in The Healing Project, ed., *Voices of Lung Cancer*. p. 192.
43. Wheresmyp53, "Killing Cancer One Cell at a Time," April 17, 2007. http://wheresmyp53.blogspot.com/2007_04_01_archive.html.

Notes

44. Quoted in Henschke, *Lung Cancer Myths, Facts, Choices—and Hope*, p. 233.
45. Quoted in Claudia Driefus,"A Hopeful Outlook on Taming Cancer," *AARP Bulletin*, December 2003, p. 13.
46. Sievers, "My Cancer," July 3, 2007.

Chapter 4: Living with Lung Cancer

47. Seivers, NPR.org, "My Cancer."
48. Henschke, McCarthy, and Wernick, *Lung Cancer Myths, Facts, Choices—and Hope*, p. 287.
49. Quoted in Henschke, McCarthy, and Wernick, *Lung Cancer Myths, Facts, Choices—and Hope*, p. 288.
50. Wheresmyp53, "Killing Cancer One Cell at a Time," September 12, 2006. wheresmyp53.blogspot.com/2006_09_01_archive.html.
51. Quoted in The Healing Project, ed., *Voices of Lung Cancer*, p. 193.
52. Lung Cancer Alliance, "Frankly Speaking about Lung Cancer, Maximizing Your Health and Well-being." www.lungcanceralliance.org/frankly/maximizing/physical_activity_and_exercise.html
53. Quoted in The Lung Cancer Survivor's Community, "What is it Like to Live With One Lung?" Comment # 13639. http://lungcancer.clinicahealth.com/comments.pl?sid=06/11/28/2128219.
54. Quoted in The Lung Cancer Survivor's Community, "What is it Like to Live With One Lung?" Comment # 11028.
55. Quoted in Johnston, *Lung Cancer Making Sense of Diagnosis, Treatment & Options*, p.184.
56. Karen Parles and Joan H. Schiller, *100 Questions & Answers about Lung Cancer*. Sudbury, MA: Jones and Bartlett Publishers, 2006. p. 158.
57. Quoted in Johnston, *Lung Cancer Making Sense of Diagnosis, Treatment & Options*, p.194.
58. Wheresmyp53, "Killing Cancer One Cell at a Time," October 2, 2006. http://wheresmyp53.blogspot.com/2006_10_01_archive.html.

59. Look Good… Feel Better, "A DreamGirl's Life." www.lookgoodfeelbetter.org/women/explore/more_stories/dream_girls_life.htm.
60. Quoted in The Healing Project, ed., *Voices of Lung Cancer*. p. 60.
61. Bass, "Faces of Lung Cancer."
62. Look Good… Feel Better, "Women with Cancer Manage Appearance Related Concerns with Help of Look Good… Feel Better," April 25, 2007. www.lookgoodfeelbetter.org/audience/pdf/LGFB_WEEK07PR.pdf.
63. Johnson, "Faces of Lung Cancer."
64. Seivers, "My Cancer," June 11, 2007.
65. Quoted in The Healing Project, ed., *Voices of Lung Cancer*, p. 44.
66. Quoted in Donna Olmstead, *Albuquerque Journal Boomer Magazine*, "Stand By Me," April 2007, p. 9.
67. Quoted in The Healing Project, ed., *Voices of Lung Cancer*, p. 118.

Chapter 5: What the Future Holds

68. Parles and Schiller, *100 Questions & Answers about Lung Cancer*, p.170.
69. Quoted in CNN.com, "CNN Larry King Live," April 25, 2005.
70. National Cancer Institute, "Questions and Answers about Smoking Cessation." www.cancer.gov/cancertopics/factsheet/Tobacco/cessation.
71. Quoted in Lisa Stark, Secondhand Smokes You.com, "Do Smoking Bans Really Get People to Quit?," *ABC World News Tonight*, November 8, 2005. www.secondhandsmokesyou.com/resources/one_news_article.php?id=116.
72. Quoted in University of Medicine and Dentistry of New Jersey, "Study Finds That New Jersey Bars and Restaurants Have Nine Times More Air Pollution than Those in Smoke-Free New York." http://www.umdnj.edu/about/news_events/releases/04/r041214_bars.htm.
73. People Living with Cancer, "Q&A: Living With Lung Cancer," November 27, 2006.

Notes

74. Quoted in Xillix, "Xillix Life-Lung." www.xillix.com/life_lungl.cfm.
75. Henschke, McCarthy, and Wernick, *Lung Cancer Myths, Facts, Choices—and Hope*, p. 2.
76. Quoted in MSNBC.com, "Breath Test Detects Most Cases of Lung Cancer." February 26. 2007. www.msnbc.msn.com/id/17345378/.
77. Quoted in Charlene Laino, Web MD, "Breath Test for Lung Cancer?," April 16, 2007. www.webmd.com/lung-cancer/news/20070416/breath-test-for-lung-cancer.
78. Medical News Today, "Vaccination with Embryonic Stem Cells Prevents Lung Cancer in Mice," November 13, 2006. www.medicalnewstoday.com/medicalnews.php?newsid=56439.
79. Quoted in The Healing Project, ed., *Voices of Lung Cancer*, p. 251.

Glossary

alveoli: The air sacs in the lungs.

asbestos: A mineral, which releases fibers that can cause the development of lung cancer.

biopsy: A sample of tissue taken from a tumor for medical analysis.

benign tumor: An abnormal mass made of non-cancerous cells.

bronchoscopy: A procedure in which a tube is inserted through the nose into the lungs in order to view the lungs and gather lung tissue for analysis.

cancer: A disease in which mutated cells grow uncontrollably without purpose or order.

carcinoma: Another word for cancer.

carcinogen: A substance that has cancer causing properties.

cell: Microscopic unit that makes up all forms of life.

computerized axial tomography scan (CT or CAT scan): An imaging device that takes three-dimensional cross-sectional pictures of a body part.

lobe: A section of the lung. The right lung has three lobes; the left has two lobes.

lobectomy: Surgical removal of a lobe of the lung.

malignant tumor: An abnormal mass made of cancerous cells.

mesothelioma: A rare type of lung cancer associated with exposure to asbestos.

metastasis: The process in which cancer cells spread from one part of the body to another.

Glossary

non-small cell lung cancer (NSCLC): The most common type of lung cancer.

oncologist: A doctor who specializes in treating cancer.

oxygen therapy: The use of an oxygen tank to assist in breathing.

pathologist: A doctor who studies and analyzes body tissue in a laboratory.

pneumonectomy: Surgery in which one lung is removed.

prognosis: An estimate of how likely the patient is to be cured, or what the patient's long-term survival chances are.

pulmonologist: A doctor who specializes in diseases of the lungs.

radiation oncologist: A doctor who specializes in treating cancer with radiation therapy.

radiation therapy: Treatment that uses high doses of x-rays and other forms of radiation to kill or damage cancer cells.

remission: Period following cancer treatment in which no evidence of cancer can be found.

respiratory therapist: A healthcare professional that evaluates, cares for, and treats patients with respiratory problems.

shedding: The process in which cancer cells break free from the tumor.

simulation: A process in which a physician prepares a patient for radiation therapy.

small cell lung cancer (SCLC): A type of lung cancer.

stage: A way to classify how far cancer has spread.

thoracic surgeon: A doctor who specializes in lung surgery.

tumor suppressor genes: Genes that signal cells to stop growing.

treatment field: The area to be treated with radiation.

video assisted thorascopy (VATS): A surgical procedure that uses a tiny camera to help the surgeon view and gather lung tissue samples.

x-ray: A form of radiation that can take an image of the inside of the body.

Organizations to Contact

American Cancer Society
1599 Clifton Rd. NE
Atlanta, GA 30329
(800) 227-2345
www.cancer.org

The American Cancer Society is a national organization with local groups throughout the country. It offers information on all types of cancer and sponsors support groups.

American Lung Association
61 Broadway, 6th floor
New York, NY 10006
(800) LUNG-USA
www.lungusa.org

The Association works to prevent all types of lung disease. It provides information, smoking prevention and cessation programs, and support.

Joan Scarangello Foundation
27 Union Square West, Suite 304
New York, NY 10003
(212) 657-5500
www.joanslegacy.org

This organization was founded in memory of Joan Scarangello who died of lung cancer. It funds lung cancer research, provides information, and has many helpful links on its website.

Lung Cancer Alliance
888 16th St. NW, Suite 800
Washington, DC 20006
(800) 298–2436
info@lungcanceralliance.org
www.lungcanceralliance.org

A national organization dedicated to advocating for people with lung cancer. It promotes fundraising and research, and provides information and support.

LUNGevity Foundation
2421 N. Ashland Ave
Chicago, IL 60614
(773) 281–LUNG
www.lungevity.org

A foundation dedicated to funding lung caner research and providing support for people with lung cancer and their families.

For Further Reading

Books
Marlene Targ Brill, *Lung Cancer*. New York: Benchmark Books, 2005. A simple look at lung cancer written for children.

Carmen Ferreiro and I. Edward Alcamo, *Lung Cancer*. Langhorne, PA: Chelsea House, 2007. A young adult book dealing with lung cancer.

The Healing Project, *Voices of Lung Cancer*. New York: LaChance Publishing, 2007. A series of essays dealing with all aspects of lung cancer written by lung cancer patients, their families, and lung cancer experts.

Julie Walker, *Lung Cancer: Current and Emerging Trends in Treatment and Detection*. NY: Rosen Central, 2005. A young adult book focusing on the detection and treatment of lung cancer.

Lisa Yount, *Cancer*. San Diego: Lucent Books, 1999. An informative book that looks at cancer in general.

Periodicals
Christine Gorman, "Lung Cancer and the Sexes," *Time Magazine*, July 16, 2006.

Bernadette Healey, "The Case for Screening," *U.S. News and World Report*, April 15, 2007.

Marc Siegel, "Stupid Cancer Statistics," *The Wall Street Journal*, March 15, 2007.

Claudia Wallis, "How to Live with Cancer," *Time Magazine*, April 9, 2007.

Internet Sources
CNN.com, "Transcripts, CNN Larry King Live Panel Discusses Lung Cancer," http://transcripts.cnn.com/TRANSCRIPTS/0504/05/lkl.01.html.

Newsday.com, "Lauren Terrazzno, Life with Cancer," www.newsday.com/ny-terrazzano-column,0,6784588.columnist.

Web sites

Lung Cancer.org, (www.lungcancer.org/) Provides information on every aspect of lung cancer including support and articles by people fighting the disease.

National Lung Cancer Partnership (www.nationallungcancerpartnership.org/main.cfm) Information about lung cancer and specifically how it affects women.

NPR.org, "My Cancer," (http://www.npr.org/blogs/mycancer/) Blog about living with cancer written for NPR by Leroy Sievers, a noted journalist who is fighting lung cancer.

Quit Net, (QuitNet.com) An internet support group for people who want to quit smoking.

Web MD, "Lung Cancer Help Center," (http://www.webmd.com/lung-cancer/default.htm) Provides a wealth of information about lung cancer including numerous links.

Index

Abdominal imaging study, 32
Accident proneness, 49
Acid reflux, 30
Acupuncture, 53
Adenocarcinoma, 37
Adrenal glands, 14
Advocacy organizations, 7
African Americans, vulnerability to lung cancer, 23
Air pollution, 20
Air sacs (alveoli), 12
Alcohol consumption, 7
Alveoli (air sacs), 12
American Cancer Organization, 66
American Cancer Society, 72
American Lung Association, 23, 71
Analysis, of cancer cells, 34–37
   bronchoscope, 36
   bronchoscopy, 35, 36
   mediastinoscopy procedure, 37
   video assisted thoracoscopy, 37
Antibiotics, inhaled, 44
Appetite
   loss of, 30, 50
   management of, 62–64
Asbestos, 15, 21–22
See also Mesothelioma
Assisted breathing, 43–44
Avon Breast Cancer 3-Day event, 9

Bass, Cindy, 28
Benign tumors, 12–13, 34
Biopsy, 34, 36
Bladder cancer, 22
Blood clots, 44
Bloodstream/blood vessels, 12
Bone injury, 30
Bones, 14

Brain, 14, 32
Breast cancer, 8, 10, 22
Breath test development, 79–81
Breathing, 12
Breathing therapy, 44
Britt, Sandy Phillips, 10, 28
Bronchi/bronchioles, 12
Bronchitis, 30
Bronchoscope/bronchoscopy, 35–36
Buck, Joe, 10

Cancer cells, 12–14
   analysis, 34–37
   biopsy, 34
   doubling time, 15
   shedding process, 14–15
Carcinogens, 15–18, 24
Carmona, Richard A., 19, 21
CAT (computer axial tomography) scan, 28, 32, 33, 36
Causes of lung cancer
   asbestos, 15, 21–22
   radon, 15, 18, 19, 21
   second hand smoke, 18
   See also Cigarette smoking
Cedar Sinai Skin Cancer Institute, 16
Cell division, uncontrolled, 11–12
Center for Tobacco Control Research and Education (UCSF), 75
Centers for Disease Control and Prevention, 22
Cessation of smoking. *See* Cigarette smoking prevention
Chemotherapy
   cyclical administration, 48–49
   drug mix, 48
   food preferences after, 63
   hydration, importance of, 62, 63

killing of red/white blood cells, 51, 52
nerve cells and, 49
pre-surgical administration, 46–47
side effects, 49, 50–52, 62
surgery vs., 47
Chest pain, 30
Children
  children's cancers, 8
  second hand smoke exposure, 19
Cigar smoking, 24
Cigarette smoking
  cessation/prevention, 17–18, 70–77
  genetic damage, 16–17
  international statistics, 74–75
  light cigarettes, 24
  lung cancer association, 6, 16
  second hand smoke, 15–16, 18
Cigarette smoking prevention, 70–77
  cessation programs, 71–73
  Great American Smoke Out, 72, 73
  Not on Tobacco program, 71–72
  support groups, 72
Clinical trials, 46, 50
Colds, 30
Collapsed lungs, 43
Colorectal cancer, 8, 22
Complementary alternative treatment, 52–54
Computer axial tomography (CAT) scan, 28, 32, 33
Cortisol (hormone), 54
Coughing, 29, 30
Coyle, Yvonne, 20
Cysts, 34

Diagnosis
  bronchoscope/bronchoscopy, 35–36
  distinguishing type/stage, 37–39
  early diagnosis, 77–79
  healthcare professional team, 34
  imaging tests, 28, 31–33

mediastinoscopy procedure, 37
misdiagnosis possibility, 31
non-small cell lung cancer, 37, 39
possibility of confusion, 29–31
small cell lung cancer, 37, 39, 40
video assisted thorascopy, 37
See also Treatment
Diagnosis, future developments
  breath test, 79–81
  DNA analysis, 81–82
  lung cancer vaccine, 82, 84
  targeted treatment vaccine, 84–85
Dietary routine, 7, 62, 63
Doubling time, of cancer cells, 15

Emotional distress, 66–67
Environmental Protection Agency, 18
Environmental toxins, 18–23
Eschenbach, Andrew C. von, 53
Esophageal burns, 51
Esophageal cancer, 24
Exercise, 44, 58–60

Fatigue, 29, 30, 50, 52, 55–56
Federal Drug Administration (FDA), 52
Fever, low-grade, 30
Food preferences, post-chemotherapy, 63
Foulds, Jonathan, 75
Fruit smoothies, 63
Future developments in diagnosis
  breath test, 79–81
  DNA analysis, 81–82
  lung cancer vaccine, 82, 84
  targeted treatment vaccine, 84–85

Gender role, 23, 25–26
Genetic damage, from smoking, 16–17
Glantz, Stanton, 75
Great American Smoke Out, 72, 73
Guided imagery, 54

Hair loss, 50, 51–52, 64–66

Index

Hand washing, 62
Headaches, 30
Herbal remedies, 53
Hoarseness, 30
Hospice care, 69
Hydration, importance of, 62, 63

Imaging tests, 28, 30–33
Immune system, 13–14
Inactivity, 7
Infections
   avoidance, 61–62
   influence of stress, 67
   respiratory/sinus infections, 30
   surgical risks, 44
   white blood cell concerns, 45
Intravenous (IV) tubes, 43, 48

Jahan, Thierry, 47

Kidney cancer, 22
Kris, Mark, 16

Large cell carcinoma, 37
Larynx, 30
"Light" cigarettes, 24
Lip cancer, 24
Liver disease, 7, 14
Living with lung cancer
   appetite management, 62–64
   breathing difficulties, 59–61
   coping with fatigue, 30, 42, 50, 55–56
   emotional distress, 66–67
   hair loss, 50, 51–52, 64
   importance of hydration, 62
   infections avoidance, 61–62
   pain management, 57–59
   support groups, 67, 69
Lobectomy, 43
Look Good… Feel Better program, 64, 66
Los Angeles, air pollution, 20
Lung cancer
   asbestos association, 15, 21–22
   description, 11–26
   development time, 17
   diagnosis, 28
   distinguishing type/stage, 37–39
   doubling time, 15
   healthcare professional team, 34
   lack of media attention, 7–8
   prognosis determination, 39–40
   radon association, 15, 18, 19, 21
   rates, 8, 17
   research funds limitations, 8, 10
   as "smoker's disease," 8
   survival rates, 10
   symptoms, 27–31
Lung Cancer Alliance, 10
Lung Cancer Online Foundation, 7
Lungs
   natural cleaning system, 16
   physiology, 12, 13
   upper right lobe diagnosis, 40
Lymph nodes, 14, 35, 43

Malignant tumors, 12–14
Massachusetts Institute of Technology (MIT) study, 24
Media, lack of attention for lung cancer, 7–8
Mediastinoscopy procedure, 37
Medication
   anti-nausea drugs, 62
   anti-nausea medication, 51
   experimental drugs, 50
   for sedation, 43
   Tarceva, 51
   throat numbing drugs, 62
Meditation, 54
Men
   commonness of lung cancer, 8
   development of lung cancer, 23, 25
Mental confusion, 49
Mesothelioma, 22
Metastasizing cancer, 30, 35
Mind/body techniques, 54
Misdiagnosis possibility, 31
Mourning, Alonzo, 73
Mouth cancer, 24
MRI imaging study, 30–31
Mueller, Scarlott, 71

Natale, Ronald, 16
National Cancer Institute, 16, 19,

53
National Institute of Environmental Health Sciences, 19
Nausea/vomiting, 50, 51, 62
Neck/shoulder pain, 30
Needle biopsy, 36
Nerve cells, and chemotherapy, 49
Nicotine, 16
Non-Hodgkin lymphoma, 22
Non-small cell lung cancer (NSCLC)
  adenocarcinoma, 37
  large cell carcinoma, 37
  squamous cell carcinoma, 37
  stages, 39
  surgical determination, 41
Not on Tobacco (N-O-T), 71–72
Nutritional support
  hydration, 62, 63
  liquid nourishment, 63
  supplementation, 53

Oncologists (cancer doctor), 34
Ovarian cancer, 8, 22
Oxygen, 12, 13, 14, 29

Parles, Karen, 8
Pathologists, 39
Peripheral neuropathy, 49
Physical inactivity, 7
Physicians
  oncologists (cancer doctor), 34
  pathologists, 39
  psychiatrists, 34
  pulmonologists (lung doctors), 34
  thoracic surgeons, 42
Pleura (membrane), 12
Pneumonectomy, 43
Pneumonia, 30, 34
Prognosis determination, 30, 10
Prostate cancer, 8, 10, 22
Psychiatrists, 34
Pulmonologists (lung doctors), 34, 35

Radiation oncologists, 34

Radiation therapy
  administration procedure, 46
  food preferences after, 63
  pre-surgical administration, 44
  safety factors, 45
  side effects, 50–52
  x-rays/gamma rays, 44–45
Radon/radon detection, 15, 18, 19, 21
Red blood cells, 51, 52
Reeves, Dana, 7
Remission and recurrence, 49–50
Research, funding limitations, 8, 10
Respiratory system, 12, 13, 30
Respiratory therapists, 34, 44
Roswell Park Cancer Institute (Buffalo, NY), 75

Scar tissue, 34
Second hand smoke, 15–16, 18, 19
Shedding process, 14–15
Side effects
  hair loss, 50, 51–52, 64–66
  minimization, through guided imagery, 54
  nausea/vomiting, 50, 51, 62
  from radiation/chemotherapy, 50–52, 62
Simonton, O. Carl, 54
Sinus infections, 30, 31
Skin cancer, 22
Sloan Kettering Memorial Hospital (NYC), 16
Small cell lung cancer (SCLC), 37
  stages, 39
  surgical determination, 41
Smoking. *See* Cigar smoking; Cigarette smoking; Cigarette smoking prevention
Social workers, 34
Spreading of cancer. *See* Shedding process
Squamous cell carcinoma, 37
Stages of lung cancer
  pathologist identification, 39
  stage III, 38
  Stage IV, 10
  surgical determination, 41

Index

Support groups, 67–68, 72
Surgical treatment, 41–44
  assisted breathing, 43–44
  chemotherapy vs., 47
  lobectomy, 43
  mediastinoscopy, 37
  NSCLC III, IV/SCLC, 41
  pneumonectomy, 43
  risks, 44
  tumor removal, 41, 43–44
  video assisted thorascopy, 37, 41
Survival rates
  breast cancer, 10
  lung cancer, 10
  prostate cancer, 10
Survivors of cancer, 7, 14, 28, 31, 36, 65–66
Swallowing troubles, 30
Symptoms
  confusion caused by, 29–31
  coughing, 29, 30
  early stages, 27
  lateness of onset, 27, 28
  swallowing troubles, 30
  tumor discovery, 28

Tarceva (chemotherapy medication), 51
Teenagers, lung cancer rates, 17
Terrazano, Lauren, 25
Thoracic surgeons, 42
Throat cancer, 24
Throat numbing drugs, 62
Tobacco Dependence Program (UNDNJ), 75
Tobacco smoke. *See* Cigar smoking; Cigarette smoking; Second hand smoke
Tongue cancer, 24
Trachea (windpipe), 12, 35
Treatment
  chemotherapy, 46–49, 50–52
  clinical trials, 46
  complementary alternative treatment, 52–54

  exercise recommendation, 44
  healthcare professional team, 34
  inhaled antibiotics, 44
  radiation therapy, 44–46, 50–52
  remission and recurrence, 49–50
  surgery, 37, 41–44
  See also Diagnosis
Tumors
  airway location, 29
  benign, 12–13, 34
  coughing blood, 30
  discovery of, 28
  imaging detection, 32
  malignant, 12–14
  pain-free growth, 27
  surgical removal, 41, 43–44
  symptoms of metastasis, 30
Type/stage of cancer, 37, 39
  non-small cell lung cancer, 37
  small cell lung cancer, 37

Uterine cancer, 22

Video assisted thorascopy (VAT), 37, 41
Vulnerability to lung cancer
  African Americans, 23
  gender, 23, 25–26

Weight loss, 30
Weill Medical College (NYC), 25
Weinberg, Robert A., 12, 13, 14
White blood cells, 14, 51, 52
Wigs, for hair loss, 66
Women
  Avon Breast Cancer 3-Day event, 9
  commonness of lung cancer, 8
  development of lung cancer, 23, 25

X-rays
  diagnostic use, 28, 31, 38
  therapeutic use, 44–45

Picture Credits

Cover: Courtesy of photos.com
Antonia Reeve/Photo Researchers, Inc., 35
AP Images, 45, 47, 51, 53, 60, 68, 71, 73, 76, 80
Charles D. Winters/Photo Researchers, Inc., 21
Custom Medical Stock Photo, Inc., 15, 78
David McNew/Getty Images News/Getty Images, 20
Dr. E. Walker/Photo Researcher, Inc., 29
Gg/eStock Photo/Jupiter Images, 6
Illustration by Hans & Cassidy. Cengage Learning, Gale, 13
© Image Source/Corbis, 19
Kevin Winter/Getty Images Entertainment/Getty Images, 9
© Peter Yates/Corbis, 42
Scott Camazine/Photo Researchers, Inc., 38
Scott Olson/Getty Images New/Getty Images, 24
Steve Liss/Time & Life Pictures/Getty Images, 17
© Tim Pannell/Corbis, 57
© 2007/Jupiter Images, 33, 58, 83

About the Author

Barbara Sheen is the author of more than 40 non-fiction books for young people. She lives in New Mexico with her family. In her spare time, she likes to swim, walk, cook, read, and garden.